Heathen

WALL STREET JOURNAL & USA TODAY BESTSELLING AUTHOR

SAPPHIRE KNIGHT

Blaze

Copyright © 2019 by Sapphire Knight

Cover Design by CT Cover Creations
Editing by Mitzi Carroll

Oath Keepers MC Series

Secrets
Exposed
Relinquish
Forsaken Control
Friction
Princess
Sweet Surrender – free short story
Love and Obey – free short story
Daydream
Baby
Chevelle
Cherry
Heathen

Russkaya Mafiya Series

Secrets

Corrupted
Corrupted Counterparts – free short story
Unwanted Sacrifices
Undercover Intentions

Dirty Down South Series

Freight Train
3 Times the Heat
2 Times the Bliss

Complete Standalones

Gangster
Unexpected Forfeit
The Main Event – free short story
Oath Keepers MC Collection
Russian Roulette
Tease – Short Story Collection
Oath Keepers MC Hybrid Collection
Vendetti
Viking - free newsletter short story

Capo Dei Capi Vendetti Duet

The Vendetti Empire - part 1
The Vendetti Queen - part 2

Harvard Academy Elite Duet

Little White Lies
Ugly Dark Truth

WARNING

This novel includes graphic language and adult situations. It may be offensive to some readers and includes situations that may be hotspots for certain individuals. This book is intended for ages 18 and older due to some steamy spots. This work is fictional. The story is meant to entertain the reader and may not always be completely accurate. Any reproduction of these works without Author Sapphire Knight's written consent is pirating and will be punished to the fullest extent of the law.

- **This book is fiction.**
- **The guys are over-the-top alphas.**
- **My men and women are nuts.**
- **This is not real.**
- **Don't steal my shit.**
- **Read for enjoyment.**
- **This is not your momma's cookbook.**
- **Easily offended people should not read this.**
- **Don't be a dick.**
- **Romance shaming is slut shaming, don't be that asshole.**

My husband – This life wouldn't be possible without having your continued support. I know it's not always easy when I zone out on my laptop and don't want to be disturbed. I appreciate you rolling with it and embracing my chosen career. I'm glad you've discovered a way to implement Knight Creations business to fit so well with mine. I wouldn't want to spend my life with anyone else. I love you, I'm thankful for you, I can't say it enough.

My boys – You are my whole world. I love you both. This never changes, and you better not be reading these books until you're thirty and tell yourself your momma did not write them! I can never express how grateful I am for your support. You are quick to tell me that my career makes you proud, that I make you proud. As far as mom wins go, that one takes the cake. I love you with every beat of my heart, and I will forever.

Editor Mitzi Carroll – Your hard work makes mine stand out, and I'm so grateful! Thank you for pouring tons of hours into my passion and being so wonderful to me. Thank you for your amazing support.

Cover Designer Clarise Tan – I cannot thank you enough for the wonderful work you've done for me. Your continued help and support truly means so much. I can't wait to see our future projects; you always blow me away. You are a creative genius!

Jay - Thank you for your support, woman! You rock! I hope you love the ARC copy. :)

My Blogger Friends – YOU ARE AMAZING! I LOVE YOU! No, really, I do. You take a new chance on me with each book and in return, share my passion with the world. You never truly get enough credit, and I'm forever grateful! There are so many of you that have stuck with me from the beginning, that dedication is truly humbling.

My Readers – I love you. You make my life possible, thank you. I can't wait to meet many of you this year and in the future. To those of you leaving me the awesome spoiler free reviews, you motivate me to keep writing. For that, I will forever be grateful, as this is my passion in life.

And as always, ADOPT DON'T SHOP! Save a life today and adopt from a rescue or your local animal shelter. **#ProudDobermanMom**

This one's for everyone who is sick of one-sided arguments and ideologies. The world is a big place, we have the right to all have our own views and thoughts. It doesn't mean you have to like it or agree, but respect is deserved from everyone. There are too many assholes out there, let's be better.

Also, if you're reading my books, then I know you're not small minded. Thank you for being one of the good ones.

(charter, road name, position, ol' lady, nickname, kids, book title)

Oath Keepers/Widow Makers hybrid charter:

Viking – President (Prez),
Heir to the Widow Makers MC, previous NOMAD,
Princess aka Cinderella - ol' lady (Princess)

Odin – Vice President (VP), Vikings younger blood brother,
previous Widow Maker, Cherry - ol' lady (Cherry)

Torch – Death Dealer (punisher/enforcer), previous Widow Maker,
grew up with Viking, Annabelle Teague - daughter

Saint and Sinner – Hell Raisers, previous NOMADS,
Jude aka Baby - ol' lady (Baby)

Nightmare – Good friend to Viking and Exterminator,
club officer, previous NOMAD, Bethany aka Daydream - ol' lady,
Maverick – son (Daydream)

Blaze – Vikings cousin and Princess' security,
previous Widow Maker
Amelia aka Teach – ol' lady (Heathen)

Chaos – Close with the NOMADS, Ex NFL football player

Smokey – Treasurer, previous Widow Maker

Mercenary – Transfer from Chicago Charter, newest officer,
Chevelle aka Chevy - ol' lady, Hemi, Nova, Shelby – son and
daughters (Chevelle)

Frost – Prospect, Bronx' blood brother
Karma – Prospect, twin to Rage
Rage – Prospect, twin to Karma
Scot – Deceased
Bronx – Deceased

NOMADS:
Exterminator
Ruger
Spider
Knuckle Buster
Magnum

Original Oath Keepers MC:
Ares – Prez, Avery - ol' lady (Forsaken Control)
Cain – VP, London - ol' lady, Jamison Cade – son (Exposed)
2 Piece – Gun Runner – SAA, Avery - ol' lady (Relinquish)
Twist – Unholy One, Sadie aka Sadie Baby - ol' lady, Cyle – son (Friction)
Spin – Treasurer
Snake – Previous President's son, Peppermint - ol' lady (Sweet Surrender)
Capone – Deceased
Smiles – Deceased
Shooter – Deceased
Scratch – Deceased

Rivals
Iron Fists MC
Twisted Snakes MC
Mexican Cartel

Clubs Mentioned
Menace Mayhem MC – Alaska Charter – **Grizzly**

Heathen – (informal use) An unenlightened person; a person regarded as lacking culture or moral principles.

Welcome to the Oath Keepers MC, where we say fuck what you think. Unless you're Blaze and a feisty principal, then all bets are off.

With her nose stuck in the air, Doctor Amelia Stone thinks she has Blaze's character pegged. He's a heathen after all, not someone she'd ever think twice about. Unbeknownst to the overconfident principal, Blaze isn't one of the weak beta males Amelia's used to intimidating. This is one biker who won't back down.

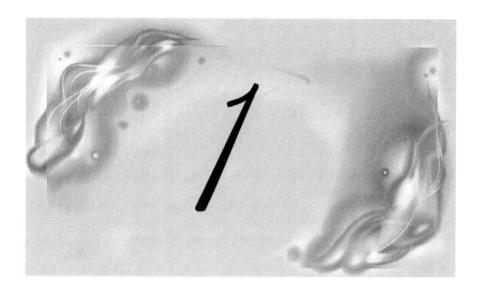

Blaze

"Well?" Torch mutters once we both get situated on the barstools at the hole-in-the-wall bar. We're close to the compound at a place that a former ol' lady owns. Her ol' man died awhile back, and we drop in from time to time to check up on her and the business. Being a biker, loyalty and family is everything. Not necessarily blood relations but rather, our MC family—the people we choose to have in our lives.

"What?" I groan and signal for a beer as Torch glares at anyone who even attempts a glance in his direction. A new bartender is working, and she's a hot little piece of ass. She's one of a few around here I haven't had yet and wouldn't mind getting my dick wet with.

"Do you have a plan with this female principal? We've discussed her a few times, and now you've got Viking and Odin both on your back about doing something with her." Torch may be a moody fuck and Viking's oldest friend, but he's also a nosey bastard. Most wouldn't know that insignificant fact about him, but being around him through the Widow Makers and now the Oath Keepers, well, I have his ass pegged. You don't become the death dealer by being an idiot. He kills people and knows shit; it's just what he does.

"You heard the brothers; they don't give two fucks what I do with her as long as I get her to heel." My VP and Prez have both ordered me to take care of this feisty woman who's been giving the club brats issues at school. Personally, I'm used to being judged and treated differently being associated with the club. The kids, however, don't deserve it. From what I've heard in church, this woman's a complete snot to anyone affiliated with the club—members included.

He snorts, his merciless gaze not believing I can make it happen. He runs his hand through his unruly hair and complains. "I've dealt with this bitch, and believe me when I say she's a cunt. You think this is going to be easy, but me an' Nightmare know damn well she's stubborn as hell with her nose so fucking high up in the air when it comes to the club that she'll put your ass through the wringer."

Flashing him a cocky grin, I take a swig of the ice-cold beer that'd been set in front of me before responding. "I'll try to be nice, work some charm on her. Hell, maybe I'll bring her some fucking flowers and let her know that if she needs anything at all, I'll be more than obliged to offer a helping hand. Chicks can't resist when I turn up the charm."

"Not going to work." He shakes his head and requests a double American Honey, chilled. It's Wild Turkey with a hint of sweetness. Torch drums his fingers on the bar top as he speaks. "She's going to look down that sharp nose of hers and flick you off like a motherfucking flea. You don't believe me, but you'll see."

With a shrug, I wave off his comment. "Then I'll knock the bitch out and kidnap her. The choice is up to her. I'll put the ball in her court and let her actions decide how I treat her." I've dealt with female club problems in the past—with the Oath Keepers as well as when I was a Widow Maker. Granted, my methods have changed a bit, but I'll still get to the nitty-gritty if required; this chick won't get the best of me.

His hand goes to his forehead, his fingers massaging his temples as he swears under his breath. Torch rarely shows emotion to anyone other than our MC brothers, and even then, it's only to those of us who used to be Widow Makers alongside him. He's learned the hard way not to trust, so I can't blame him for being the cold fucker he is today. "You'll end up in jail. She's the type to press charges, and being a biker, she won't hesitate to take your ass to court. Tread easy with this one...-a quick in and out," he warns, and it's my turn to scoff.

"I'm gonna mow that bitch over before she has a clue what's happened. I'm coming from left field, unannounced and unexpected. She's not used to real men—of that, I'm certain. It's about time that she learns alphas aren't the motherfucking enemy. We're here to protect and provide for our women, not hurt them or oppress them."

Torch nods, taking a hefty swig of the smooth amber whiskey and leaves the subject to rest. As he sets his tumbler on the bar, I catch the tattoo of his daughter's birthday along his wrist. I'd asked about it when he'd had the tattoo done; I was curious why he chose that spot. He'd said it's a reminder, set in an area he'll see every time he makes a kill. He wants to remember the day she was born and why he eventually chose to become an Oath Keeper. He'd made the change for her—to offer her a chance at an easier life and to become a better man for her. I respect him a lot for it, too; it's easy to be selfish. Sometimes doing the right thing can be much more difficult.

The cute new bartender comes to a stop in front of me again, tipping her red head toward the bottle sitting in front of me. "Can I get you anything else, Blaze? Another beer or maybe a shot?"

I meet her hazel gaze, taking in her overly mascaraed lashes and button nose. She blushes as I murmur, "Anything?" I flash a grin, the one that women always seem to fall for. This chick makes it way too easy for me.

She tucks a strand of hair behind her ear and smiles, clarifying, "Anything else to drink?"

"Darlin', you wound me. You offer me anything and then go and pull the panties right out of my reach."

She giggles at my flirting and Torch groans. He's heard me say the same thing to every new bartender we come across. Why change it if it works? Women seem to love my personality and easy smile, and when they catch a glimpse of my abs, they love me even more.

"Come on, Mr. Fucking Casanova; my little girl's about to get out of school, and it's the perfect time for you to meet this stick-up-her-ass principal. She'll get you out of this mood, that I'm certain."

Another thing I respect about Torch; he hardly drinks in case his daughter needs him. It must be difficult living the life we've chosen, doing the deeds we're sometimes forced to do and not being buzzed through any of it. There are plenty of nights I've begun with dancing on the bar and then wake up the next day not remembering shit. I like to party; what can I say?

"Fine," I huff, suddenly not looking forward to the impending fight that's sure to come. I spare one last grin toward the cute bartender as she slides a piece of paper next to my beer and then moves on to help the next customer. With a glance at it, I can't help but chuckle and send her a wink. It's her number along with <u>ANYTHING</u> written and underlined. She has no idea what she's signing up for, but I like it.

"Ridiculous," Torch drones, watching me stuff the number in my jeans pocket as we leave the bar and hop on our bikes. He could have pussy anytime he wanted if he learned to crack a smile here and there. He'd rather brood and slit throats than fuck a harem of willing chicks; personally, I prefer getting my dick wet.

An easy fifteen-minute ride later, and we're pulling up at the school. The parking lot's littered with various cages as parents line up to load in their kids. I could drive a truck occasionally, but driving those damn vans or other cages would make me crazy. We walk our bikes back into a spot, parking next to each other. Torch likes to get off and head up to the building to get his daughter. He always wants a few minutes to ask about her day before the ride home, where the pipes drown out her soft-spoken voice. I feel for the day she finally brings a boy home to meet him. Her daddy will put some sort of fear in the kid—if he doesn't decide to just filet him on the spot.

He garners my attention, muttering, "She's the uptight one over there." He chin-lifts toward the right, and my gaze easily follows, used to his direction.

The woman's exactly as I was expecting. Her hair's up, twisted in some sort of fancy wrap style. It reminds me of when rich bitches get dressed up for dinner in movies or whatever. Her back's held ramrod straight, with a small ass encased in an expensive pants suit. She turns around, offering me a glimpse of that perfectly straight nose Torch had previously commented on, and I draw in a stunned breath.

She's so goddamn beautiful, it makes my chest ache. It's kind of like biting into a freshly baked, flaky, golden-crusted cherry pie, only to discover it has far too much sugar. Cherry pie is supposed to be a bit sweet but also have a hint of tartness. This bitch is a full-on toothache just waiting to happen. I can already tell she's going to be a bittersweet mistake of mine in some type of way.

My steps falter, as my confidence is unexpectedly a bit shaken. I was expecting her to be a plain Jane run-of-the-mill woman. I knew she'd have the legendary stick up her ass, but after witnessing her beauty, well, it puts this on an entirely different level. I'd planned to swoop in and spread a touch of the Blaze charm onto her unsuspecting ass. But, now I know that won't work. I'm sure she's been hit on since she was sixteen years old if I had to guess.

If I go in there with flowers and flirting, she'll chew me up and spit me out. I'm guessing someone fucked her up when she was younger to make her so uptight. If I'd been around, I'd blame myself. My sixteen- and seventeen-year-old self broke hearts left and right back then. I was a cocky asshole. However, I was in the Carolinas back then, so it wasn't me. I'd damn sure like to come across the idiot that did her in, though; he's the dipshit that's to blame for making this job hard on me.

"Don't think I should talk to her today," I admit with a mumble to Torch's back. He throws a glance my way and shrugs, keeping his stride toward his kid. As soon as his sweet girl sees us, she sprints in our direction.

She plows into Torch, enveloping him in a fierce hug and rambles excitedly, "Dad! I missed you today, and you brought Blaze? So cool!"

"I missed you, too, angel." He holds her pressed to his stomach as she doesn't quite hit his chest yet.

"Hey, pumpkin!" I beam a bright smile at her excited grin.

We're interrupted by a proper sounding, "Young lady! Excuse me, you can't run across the pick-up lane like that!" The principal comes to stand in front of us, and I find myself swallowing as I take her in from head to toe. She's fine as hell and more so up close.

"Excuse me, Mr...." She huffs at my brother, not appearing intimidated in the slightest.

"Torch," he growls, and she rolls her eyes. I've seen people literally shake when pegged with his glare, but not her. This is going to be interesting watching her around the MC brothers; that's for certain.

"Right. I had forgotten that we'd gotten into a previous disagreement at our last meeting about legal names. Mr....Torch, your daughter can't run through traffic," she explains, exasperated. "She could get injured or worse, be hit by a moving vehicle."

And if someone was stupid enough to hurt a hair on her head, they'd be dead. My brother would make sure of it. I have no doubt.

His brow does this tiny irritated twitch. "No one was moving. Your yuppie over there has the stop sign held up to those cages in line," Torch supplies, and I find myself grinning. He rarely speaks so politely to anyone, and witnessing him on his best behavior is amusing.

"Regardless," she shakes her head, "it's unacceptable."

Torch growls, murder overtaking his menacing stare, and I can't hold back my laugh any longer. At my interruption, the woman trains her piercing gaze on me, watching as I flick my irises over her again. Her cheeks heat at my obvious attention, and her temper spikes.

"Do you find this amusing, Mr...."

"Blaze," I reply, flashing a devious grin, dimples on full display as I saunter a step closer. Invading her personal space throws her off-kilter enough that Torch and his daughter take off for his bike. "Or...*big* daddy, Mr. sexy-as-*fuck*, hot stuff, abs of steel...any of those would work just fine, sugar." An average woman would smile, even giggle or reach out to touch my flexed bicep. I'm peacocking like a motherfucker, and it doesn't even phase this lady one bit.

Rather than giving in, she steps even closer, to the point that my steel-toed boots and the tips of her fancy heels are touching. The top of her head barely reaches my chin, but she's got such big lady balls, it feels as if she's staring eye to eye with me. If she were taller, our noses would be brushing, no doubt. "Mister Blaze." Her voice hardens, lacing with unrelenting smugness. "I don't believe you have a student enrolled here; therefore, you're trespassing. Shall I call school security to escort you to the property line?" Her head tilts to the side, basically mocking, believing she has the upper hand.

My grin turns lethal, my irises shining with challenge. "Only if you want to witness me break rent-a-cop's hands in front of all these innocent children. I came to greet my niece with her father, but they've gone, so I'll go for now."

"Until you're on her contact card for approved visitors, it'd be in your best interest to remain off school property. It's my duty to keep these children safe."

Leaning down, my nose nearly grazes hers; I get close enough to show her she doesn't intimidate me in the slightest. "I'd be happy to contact my friend, the sheriff, if you're ever concerned about their safety." Standing back up to my full height, I send her a parting wink and stride to my bike.

Torch and his daughter are waiting on me before they leave, his engine already idling. His eyebrow raises in a silent question, but I shake my head and climb on, starting my motorcycle up with a loud rumble. I rev it a few times, knowing the principal is staring her fill. She'll be touching herself later as she remembers the sound and thinks back to all the things she could've said but didn't. I don't doubt that for one minute.

Blaze

Church

"Brothers..." Viking, our club prez, looks around the table at each of us. "We've spoken about the heroin coming in over the border. I have an update from the Nomads. They're in place and keeping watch at the time until we're ready to bring some heat on the cartel. Right now, we gotta focus on breaking in these new prospects and getting the other clubs on board as backup."

Nightmare sits forward, the subject instantly infuriating him. "I'm ready to ride any fucking time of the day or night. Already told my ol' lady to prepare for it. We should be with the Nomads, not breaking in a bunch of yellow-bellied fucks."

It takes everything in me not to burst out with a chuckle. This is serious, and it'll piss off my cousin and Nightmare if I laugh. I've always used humor to deal with shit, though. I only got dubbed "Blaze" from smoking my share of weed when I was younger and getting the flames tatted on my arms. Besides, "giggles" isn't a hardcore biker name, and my uncle's Widow Makers MC wasn't a place for pussies. The Oath Keepers MC isn't either, but shit isn't quite as twisted in this MC as it was in the former.

"I'm ready, too, Night, but we're sticking to the plan. Speaking of..." Prez turns to me. "You get shit sorted out yet with the school?"

"I spoke to her," I share, not keen to tell him how it went. The brothers will be all too happy to find out that I've met a woman who's not easily bent to my charms. I'd get shit for days from them, and I'm not in the mood to deal with it, even if it is good-natured.

His brow rises, impatiently waiting for details. The man's face is like a slab of granite, fierce in every expression. I've had to face his anger in the past, and it wasn't fun. Thought I'd die that day. It works to his advantage; fewer people will fuck with an MC if the prez looks like he'll pop off your head with his bare hands and not flinch. Viking's big ass could do it, too.

Exhaling, I meet his stare and confess, "She threatened to have me removed from school property. I need Torch to add me to his daughter's approved visitors list."

Torch and Nightmare huff; both had previous run-ins with the woman, while the other brothers either smirk or outright chuckle. *The dirty bunch of bastards.* I'd like to see them do any better this early on. They sent me in to charm her; they've gotta give me a chance to do that much.

I've got Odin, my cousin, who's Viking's younger brother and our VP beside me, then sits Viking, who's my other cousin and Prez. After Prez is Torch, the club's death dealer and finally, Nightmare, an original member and one of Viking's closest friends. This end of the thick slab of oak is full of grouchy, broody fuckers, unlike the other half. The opposite side of the table seats Sinner and Saint, the club's hell raisers; Chaos, Smokey, the club treasurer, and lastly, Mercenary, our newest patched transfer from the Chicago charter up north.

Thankfully, the prospects aren't allowed in church—only the club officers—or we'd really be packed in. It's hard enough to breathe in this room with everyone smoking weed or puffing on cigarettes that, when we have visiting members, half are forced to stand against the walls. When Viking built this place, I don't think he was anticipating having one of the largest active charters in the Oath Keepers MC. If we keep growing like we have been, he may need to think of expanding the compound. We could move church into the bar, use this room for storage or something, and then build on a new, bigger bar for everyone to use. I need to stop watching the HGTV channel; it's making me want to build shit, and I don't have time for it.

Mercenary speaks up, his deep throaty rasp commanding attention. "Why don't we just have this chick replaced if she keeps causing this much shit at the school? It seems smart to me that we introduce more of our own into the fold around the compound. You've got Scot's ol' lady with the bar down the road; it's convenient to have her keeping a lookout for any incoming. My ol' lady owns the local track and can store shit for us when needed." He gestures off to the side in the general direction of his wife's business. We all stare, waiting to hear where he's going with this. It seems like a good idea if it's feasible.

Glancing around, Mercenary continues. "The Oath Keepers has a doc on payroll inside the clinic, besides 2 Piece putting in his free time patching us up. Spin's got that tattoo shop which connects him to a lot of the younger people around here, as well as the seasoned birds. Twist does all that bodywork and painting with Spin whenever a local has a custom car or bike. You've got Princess and Avery, who help by taking care of the compounds and the club sluts when needed. Odin's ol' lady does all that baking for the farmer's market downtown, which people can't seem to buy quick enough...why not branch out farther and have someone at the school too? If you think about it, the more we're integrated into the community, the more they accept us."

Viking relaxes back, his gaze beating down on Merc. Finally, he glances around, his expression lightening a touch. "Damn good idea. Any of you have a woman wanting work, or if you get one in the future, make sure she's trying to get a job at one of the places around us. Smokey, I'll get with you later to discuss our account balance and what we may be able to buy into locally. It's about time we start thinking of the future in ways we haven't already. I'm not talking about the money we bring in now, but something the club kids can have a piece of. Maybe a sandwich shop or something... I want them to have a way to be legit and not face bullshit bias harassment because they're tied to us."

I guzzle the rest of my beer, then ask, "So, I give up on the principal then? We just replacing her?"

Everyone's attention falls to me again, and Viking scoffs. "Fuck no. Plan's still in place with her. We don't have the school board on speed dial to fire her ass, so get in there and get her to submit. She's been a fucking pain to the club for long enough."

Sweat breaks out across my brow at his words, but I nod regardless. They haven't seen how fucking gorgeous she is. They're like me, assuming she's some uptight, boring, rule-enforcing, lonely cat lady. This is not the case at all; she probably turns down assholes while pumping gas or buying groceries.

"Anything else?" Prez questions, and we grunt out various no's. "Then, get the fuck out!" He slams the gavel down, and we shuffle out, headed for the bar in the next room.

Torch approaches, folding his thick, tattooed arms over his chest. "So, the chat you had with her the other day was that bad, huh?" He's fucking jack diesel; we should've called him Terminator or some shit. Back then, we had no idea how huge he'd become, though.

I nod. "I was gonna hit you up about it, but Princess has had me busy fixing her car. Viking's had too much shit going on to do it, and I don't like thinking of her without transportation." Vike's ol' lady has become the little sister I never had. I've protected her since the day after the Widow Makers MC, and I had held her hostage. She could've had her ol' man kill me, but she saved my life instead. I vowed from that moment on that I would do whatever I could to keep her safe. The vow evolved from a protection detail to her becoming my family and someone I'd consider a best friend.

"Did you get the car finished?" He sits on the stool next to mine, our broad shoulders making up a wall of muscle.

"Yeah. There was a coolant leak. Three hoses and a water pump later, and it runs like new. Pain in the fucking ass too."

A beer is placed in front of me, along with a bottle of water for Torch. I nod my thanks to Frost, the prospect working the bar today. I had to train him, so I've been around Frost more than anyone else around here lately. He's not too bad; he'll make a good club member someday.

"We can pop smoke in a few, and I can get you added onto the approved list before I take care of some club shit. She's a ballsy bitch, giving you the boot for that shit."

"Bet," I respond and take a long pull from the ice-cold beverage. I should grab some flowers or some shit and just get this over with. It's probably a good idea to make my presence known to her as much as possible. She's gotta learn real quick that she can't get rid of me so easily. I'm going to be like a fly on her ass, hard to swat away and always buzzing to remind her I'm there.

Finishing off our drinks, we throw a quick munch on some lasagna that Princess was kind enough to make for the club's lunch and head for the parking lot. As the heavy door closes behind us, a matte black Hell Cat pulls to a stop, doors opening wide to reveal the ol' ladies from the other charter.

London gets out of the driver's seat; she's tall with big tits nearly spilling over her low-cut leopard-print top. She's so damn curvy that the woman could make a man weep with her wide hips. Her hair's black as night, tinted with blue, and the outfit she's wearing has her looking every ounce of a pinup doll stepping from a magazine cover. She's a bad bitch, the ol' lady to the VP down the road, and she's almost always knocked up. Who can blame a brother, though? I'm sure we'd all have her ass on lock-down if we were in his shoes.

Avery steps from the passenger side, her auburn hair cut perfectly in layers and shining. Her nose is peppered with freckles that have her appearing a touch more innocent than she is. She comes from a wealthy home and wears money with class. She flashes an easy smile at us while looking damn good in a silk shirt she'd refer to as a blouse, no doubt. She's always in tight-as-fuck diamond-studded jean shorts that make her ass look like you could bounce a quarter off it. Not that any of us would ever go there; she's like our Jude, claimed by two of our brothers. Surprisingly, she balances their charter prez and gun runner flawlessly. She could easily use her club status to her advantage but doesn't; she's kind, welcoming, and loyal—all traits we want in an ol' lady of the Oath Keepers.

A tiny blonde climbs out of the back seat. Her hair's so light, it's nearly white and falls to her waist. She's pushing maybe five feet at most, reminding me of a pixie; she's the Oath Keepers' very own Tinker Bell. She may seem sweet and an easy target, but she's Twist's ol' lady, Sadie. He's one of the craziest motherfuckers in the entire club—the unholy one—so Sadie must be a secret badass. Not only that, but her older brother is 2 Piece, the gun runner. She's also part of the reason why I was nearly killed trying to protect Princess and our club a while back. Her kid is the grandson to the president of the Iron Fists MC, a rival of ours. I've learned that sometimes the sweetest women are the most deceptively dangerous.

"Ladies," I call out in welcome, always the charmer.

Two additional cages and a street bike pull in to park next to the Hell Cat. Bethany, Nightmare's ol' lady, gets out of a car to greet Mercenary's ol' lady in the grumbling, fully restored Nova. Chevelle owns the race track down the road, so she's always in a souped-up muscle car with enough horsepower to make you want to check the size of your balls. The crimson-haired, leather-clad female climbing off the street bike to stand beside London is Snake's ol' lady, Peppermint. This is a prime example why so many of us are single still. How can we find a chick worthy when you compare them to the bad bitches of the Oath Keepers? These females would eat the average woman alive if offered the chance.

"Fuck," Torch mutters under his breath, taking in the gorgeous group of women. "The fuck is going on?" he asks loud enough so only I can overhear him.

"Don't know, brother," I reply. "But a group of bitches this bad...in one place has me wondering if we should leave at all. Maybe we should check their cars for dynamite or some shit; they could be up to something. Viking may need us, after all."

He snorts, folding his arms across his chest, his tattooed biceps bulging as he glares at the females in front of us. "There a problem?" he asks outright. Any other group of chicks would tuck tail and get out of here, but not these troublemakers.

London saunters toward us first with a sway in her hips; the others are quick to follow. Smirking, my dimples come out to play as I tease, "Your ol' man know you stole his car again?"

She rolls her eyes, her throaty voice nearly making my cock harden as she argues. "Loretta's my car, Blaze. Besides, what's he gonna do? Spank me? Maybe you should tattle on me, after all."

"Right," I huff and shake my head. We all know she's guilty of taking off in his car for joyrides and gets the other ladies to tag along on her expeditions. If Cain weren't such a mean motherfucker, he'd never hear the end of the teasing about his ol' lady making him hunt her down when she's feeling froggy.

Chevelle grins wickedly. "You know, London, I own the track down the way...you ever want to race that pretty girl, you just let me know, hun. We'll have some fun."

Torch's and my brows rise, not wanting to bear witness to their plans that'll no doubt cause their men to worry. The door opens behind us, and Princess and Jude poke their heads out. "Ladies! You're here, come on!"

I catch Princess's wrist, halting her. "P, the fuck's goin' on? Should I stay?"

She beams a smile and shakes her head. "We're having margaritas. We decided to make it a weekly thing to meet up. You guys go; we have the prospects here to make us drinks."

Torch mumbles, but being around him so often, I catch his quick inhale of "Lord help us."

"Agreed, brother," I comment, giving Princess's wrist a soft squeeze. "Call if you need anything; I mean it."

She pats my cheek gratefully. "I will. Thank you." With that, she steps back, holding the door open, and the women step around us, heading inside.

"The brothers are in for a surprise," I say as we head for our bikes.

"The brothers are about to shit," Torch retorts, and we fire our engines up.

I grin until we hit the highway, 'cause that shit's hella funny.

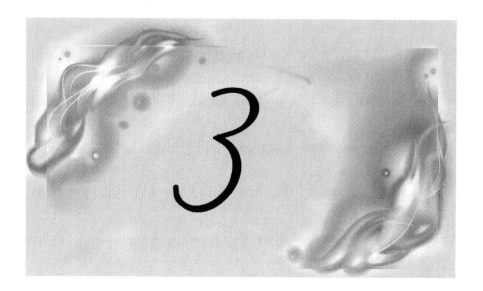

Blaze

"Can I help you, gentlemen?" The front desk lady stares wide-eyed at Torch and me, tapping her pen on the desk nervously. She's probably pushing sixty-five with her perfectly coifed hairstyle, the white having a pale sheen of pink to it. Her shirt proclaims she's a proud grandma, and I like her immediately. She's got some spunk in there; I can already tell.

Plucking the biggest daisy from my flower bunch, I present it to her with a charismatic smile. "Yes, ma'am, you sure can. I'm here to get on my niece's visitor log or whatever it's called."

"The emergency contact card and approved pick-up list," Torch mutters beside me. Apparently, he already knows these things. I have no clue. Hell, his daughter's not even my real niece, but what the school doesn't know, won't hurt.

"Of course, what's the sweet girl's name? And I'll need to see some identification, please."

He digs into his back pocket, pulling his chained wallet free and hands over his driver's license. "Her name is Annabelle Teague."

The lady glances at the ID and hands it back before heading for some stacks of papers on the shelves behind her. "We have it on the computer, but you'll need to sign a form so I can add it to her file." As she's turning to bring the paper to Torch, the door off to the left side of the room opens.

I swear it's like the first time I'm seeing this woman all over again. My chest tightens, I'm short of breath, and my cock semi-hardens. That's just from a fucking glance at the bitch too. I think if I were to hear her say the word cock or pussy, I'd come in my pants. Swallowing down my nerves, I grit my teeth to get my bearings. She can't know that she shakes me up like this; I must gain control. She's been top dog amongst her peers for far too long, and it's time she learns to humble herself with the Oath Keepers. Viking doesn't take kindly to folks getting in our way, whether it's the MC or the club brats.

The older lady brightens. "Ah, Amelia, I was just about to order your lunch, ma'am."

"Thank you, Florence. Was there an issue here?" She gestures to Torch and me. She automatically assumes something's going on, just because we're standing here, buff, bearded, tatted up, and wearing our leather cuts. She should be happy to have us at her school. It means we'd protect it if the need ever arose. God forbid they ever go on lock-down for whatever reason, but with Annabelle and Maverick around, we'd be the first to arrive to help.

Florence sets the fresh-cut daisy down on her desk and leans in and pats my cheek as I flash her another grin. "Not with these sweet boys," she replies before taking her seat. Torch fills out the form, and I arrogantly smirk at the principal. I don't even have to open my mouth, and I already drive her a bit batshit crazy.

"Don't think we've *officially* met," I say, and she sighs, her dainty hand fluttering to rub her temple.

"Mr...."

"Blaze."

"Of course," the stunning pissed off woman mutters and gestures toward the room she just came from. "May I speak to you in my office, Mr. Blaze?"

I'm not an idiot; I know damn well it's not a question. I spent most of my days in school in trouble. They always ask you nicely before they pull you in their offices and cut you down. Newsflash for this bitch; I'm not some pussy-ass beta boy nobody. I'm an Oath Keeper, and if she thinks she can rattle me, she's got another thing coming.

Closing the door behind me, she doesn't bother sitting down before she lays into me. "Do I need to remind you of our conversation yesterday? I will have you removed from school property."

Hiking my thumb toward the door, I look her over, smugly mentioning, "My boy Torch is out there right now, adding me to the approved list you mentioned, so I'm not trespassing." Stepping forward, I toss the flowers on her desk and fold my arms over my chest. "A motherfucking peace offering." I nod to them. "Now, smile and say thank you, and then I'll be on my way."

Her cheeks warm, flushing bright red. I'm not sure if she realizes it's happening or not, but I love knowing the effect my words have on her. "*Watch. Your. Mouth!*" she hisses, and I chuckle.

"You're a real stickler for the rules, aren't you, sweetheart?"

"My name is Amelia Stone—Doctor Amelia Stone. You shall address me as such."

"I'll address you as pussy lips if I see fit, especially if you continue to have that rod stuck up your ass. I think it's why your lips look so pinched, and you walk funny. I can help ya out if you'd like?" I shrug nonchalantly, and she screeches with outrage.

"Get out! Out!" Her slender finger points to the door, and I laugh, pleased to witness her lose control of her calm, cool facade.

"Already? But we've only just met—*officially*, that is."

She inhales a deep breath, attempting to gain her composure, a pacifying smile coming to rest on her lips. She thinks she's smarter than me, better than me...I can see it in her patronizing expression. "Mr. Blaze, *please* exit my office and this school, for that matter. Your language is inappropriate for children."

Dusting my nails against my shirt, I glance at them, not a care in the world when it comes to her and argue, "We're not around any children." I lean my hip against her desk, making myself comfortable.

The action further irritates her. She huffs. "I'm well aware, but you still need to leave, and now, please."

"Look, Amelia, I'm not one to go around bursting fairy tale bubbles, but you need to get used to me. We'll be seeing each other quite often."

"Oh? How do you figure?"

I step a bit closer, just enough to crowd her and smell a soft flowery scent. She thinks she's a hard bitch, but she screams woman all over. I confide, "Babe, the Oath Keepers make multiple private donations all the time. We figure this is a good stage to make sure that's well-known since we have multiple club brats going here now and in the past."

Her brow wrinkles as she opens her mouth to speak, but I interrupt. My hand reaches out, lightly grazing her sharp, pale jawline. "Annabelle and Maverick both speak highly of you."

I lie through my teeth. I've heard nothing but complaints about her from the club. However, you can catch more bees with honey I've come to learn over the years.

She flinches back, stunned I've gotten that close, and she either allowed it unconsciously or else she didn't see it coming. "I'm not at liberty to discuss students with you."

"Of course not, and you don't need to, sweetheart. We all chat about you behind your back anyhow, so we're aware of what goes down around here."

Her fingers flutter up to her temples. She's trying not to flip her shit, and I love every minute of it. Knowing I can unnerve her is all the reassurance I need at the moment to keep me going.

"I think it's best if you leave now." She repeats her earlier demand, and I can't help but fuck with her a touch more.

"Say please," I murmur, tilting my head, and her shocked stare meets mine.

"Ex-excuse me?"

"You want me to leave, say please."

She swallows, irises blazing. She's probably biting her tongue to keep from lashing out like I want her to. "Fine..." Amelia concedes, whispering, "please leave."

"Blaze," I grin, and her mouth drops open. "Say, *please leave my office, Blaze.*"

"I swear, I'll..."

"You'll what, Principal Stone?"

"Please leave my office, Blaze," she repeats. I think her head may explode if I keep pushing her right now.

My grin turns conceited, flicking my gaze over her again. "Good girl," I rasp as I turn for her door. I don't have to look at her to know she wants to throw something at my back, probably her fancy paperweight. She won't do it, but getting under Amelia's skin that much is exactly what I was hoping for.

Now I need to charm Miss Stone's schedule from sweet old Florence and start showing up enough to finally break through to the good principal. She may not know it yet, but she'll be mine. The bitch is far too feisty to not be on the back of a bike—*my bike.*

Rage and Karma greet Torch and me at the gate as we make it back to the compound. They're some of our newest prospects, a set of twins aching to belong in the club. "What are you two shitheads doing out here?" We pull to a stop, waiting for them to open the gate so we can get back to the clubhouse.

One of them, I'm not sure which since they both look the same to me, flashes a wicked grin. "Prez thought we were flirting with the ol' ladies."

The other lookalike jumps in. "Threatened to knock our teeth out and then put us on gate duty as punishment."

The first brother finishes. "Told us to be on guard since all the ol' ladies were in one place, and their safety is the most important."

Jesus, it might be a good idea in the future to have these idiots wear name tags, rather than just their vest that only has a prospect patch. It worked in the past, but when you have the same face on two people, it gets a little confusing. Why couldn't we come across twin club whores instead? Now, that, I could get on board with.

Torch nods at the younger men; he knows them better than any of us since they're his cousins. "We'll be more vigilant here on out. Shit's goin' down, so be prepared." With that, he rides through the now open gate, and I follow.

It's easy for me to get distracted and push this bullshit heroin business aside when I have a gutsy woman to deal with. Torch isn't lying about shit hitting the fan; our club despises heroin and sex trafficking, especially when it's coming into our state. Our club's been recruiting from all over. Mercenary came to us from Chicago, and some of us are from the Carolinas. Chaos is from Alabama or some shit. We're an oversized group of misfits who've come to love the state of Texas along with our club. The charter down the road is made up of born and bred Texans, who've taken to us like family, and we protect what's ours—family, friends, and the state.

"You think they'll lose the prospect cuts anytime soon?" I gripe to my brother once we park and head inside.

"Doubtful, they're too new. Why?" he grumbles back.

"'Cause I can't for the life of me figure out which motherfucker is Rage and which is Karma."

He smirks. "Rage has the smoker's voice."

"They both seem rough to me." I shrug and head for Viking's office.

"Nah, if you pay attention, you can hear it. His vocal cords were damaged."

"The fuck?" I probe, and his hands clench into fists.

"Some shit he went through as a kid. My aunt was pretty fucked in her head and put those two through hell."

I leave it alone and hit my fist against the open door to announce our presence. "Prez?"

"Mm?" Vike grunts.

"Figured you'd be out drinking margaritas with the women." We chuckle, and each takes a seat on the old broken-in couch adjacent to Viking's desk.

He broods. "Laugh, motherfucker, but I've seen your ass drunk on those damn frou-frou drinks my ol' lady throws together." He's got braids along the crown of his head, leading into a ponytail with the rest of his head shaved. It's standard for the men in our family to have similar hair. We're all blond, and with us always out riding in the sun, it lightens the various pale shades. We represent our Nordic heritage with our light features and big frames.

Rolling my eyes, my legs stretch out in front, my chunky, steel-toed boots weighing my feet down as my hands go behind my neck.

The couch is comfy; we've all slept on it at least once. "You gonna tell us what the next step is in this cartel bullshit that's goin' down?"

Torch folds his arms over his chest, his broad shoulders nearly encroaching on my space. "You ought to have me go in alone and take a good chunk of those cocksuckers out before they know what the fuck has hit them."

Vike's brow lifts. He shifts back in his office chair, staring both of us down. "They fuck you up, and I have no way to get you out. They kill you, and I'm down a death dealer." It's not the answer Torch was wanting, but he shouldn't be asking to go in the first place.

I butt in. "You've got Annabelle, brother."

His glare shifts from Viking to me, and my shoulders shrug, unperturbed. I've known these two damn near my entire life. I'm well aware that they're a couple of cruel motherfuckers. Doesn't mean I'll shrink when they get irritated. "I can probably get to their boss without them ever knowing we were coming for them. I wouldn't suggest it if I thought Annabelle would be left fatherless."

Viking grumbles. "Then you're a fucking idiot, Torch. Those Mexicans are fucking sly when it comes to their cartel business, and they'd find you out somehow. We'll let the Nomads keep watch, and if they catch onto something they can't handle, they'll hit us up."

"They helping out with border patrol down there?" I ask. We rarely work with any police unless they're on our payroll. Sometimes, however, in cases like this where the assholes are affecting us all, we step up and see what we can offer.

He shakes his head and mouths 'ICE.' "You know we don't get involved," he replies louder, making me wonder if our conversation's being monitored somehow. We sweep for bugs regularly and keep watch for anyone around the compound. We learned the first time our space was breached. Hell, I damn sure learned my lesson after nearly dying because of the Iron Fists. Maybe he's concerned about some of the newer people around or the ol' ladies visiting. I should've closed his door.

"Torch, we get called to ride, I want you here with the prospects. Last time it was Blaze, and he got fucked up, but I think with you and the others, you'll have a better chance at protecting the compound."

My mouth falls open. "You don't want me with P?" I'm shocked; it's always been my thing to protect his ol' lady, above all else.

"I want you riding with the club where you should be. Torch will watch out for her safety; besides, the bitch is pretty good with a Glock nowadays. We load her up, and anyone coming for her will take a hit, you know damn well."

He's right; she nearly shot his ass when she was pissed. I almost took a bullet trying to get the damn gun away from her. Those two are crazy when they lose it, especially when it comes to them as a couple. Still, I can't help but worry. Torch is ruthless, but Princess has become the sister I never had. I would filet anyone who wanted to harm a hair on her pretty little head, and Torch better do the same in my place.

"Right now, we have various brothers and the club whores making sure we're prepared here as well as for an unexpected ride. I want you concentrating on the school, namely that mouthy principal. It's time to take care of the less pressing shit so we can focus on the big issue that's about to be knocking at our doors."

Torch grunts, and I place my hands on my jean-clad thighs, leaning forward a bit. "I razzed her up a bit today. I'm going to start showing up every day, so she understands I'm not backing off."

"Just take the bitch and tie her up somewhere," he moodily suggests, and my hands go up, placating.

"I'm going to give her a few days to see if she'll come around. If not, I'll get something from the doc...a knockout drug, so I can take her without a struggle. I'll have to keep her in my room unless you know of a better place, somewhere she won't be overheard easily."

"Nah." He shakes his head, muttering. "Just play it safe and bring her here. If she gets loose somehow, then someone around here will be available to help catch her. When it's time, take a truck and get one of the brothers to help if you need it."

"All righty." I stand and step for the door. *So much for taking it easy with her, I suppose.* "I'll make it happen." I fist bump him and nod to Torch as well on my way out. I was planning to be sweet on her, but Viking's impatient. Now it's time to come up with a plan to kidnap her gorgeous ass. I need to figure out a way to do it and not make her completely hate me in the process. Though makeup sex can be fun, maybe she'll be into it...I'll soon be finding out.

Amelia

"Amelia?"

My gaze snaps toward Florence as I leave my office. "Yes?"

Crossing the room, I step around the few extra desks behind the parent wall. We have a barrier between us and the check-in/waiting area. It's essentially one long bookshelf with a countertop, nothing fancy but helps hide the various manuals we're required to keep up front, as well as a vast selection of printed school forms and supplies.

"You have a lunch meeting scheduled today. I wanted to let you know since it was a last-minute addition to your calendar. Would you like me to order you something to eat from that organic place you enjoy so much?" Her wrinkled hand lightly fluffs at her short, pink-tinted puffy hair.

She's in another T-shirt her grandkids made for her, and the sight makes me smile. She truly loves her job and having the chance to be around so many children. I've never met someone so family-oriented before. Her presence makes me long for my own grandmother, God rest her soul. She was the best woman I've ever known. I'm lucky to have someone close by that reminds me of her.

"I'll just have a salad from the cafeteria when I have a free minute, but thank you. What was the reason for the last-minute appointment? Was it a particular student or something?"

I was looking forward to a few minutes by myself to recharge. It's been one thing after another this week so far, it seems. I've had to deal with angry parents because grades weren't updated in the online system just yet, even though they technically aren't due until Friday at four o'clock. Then there were a couple of fifth graders who thought it would be a good idea to use their fists on each other versus talking out their issues. Those parents were so upset, one was threatening to sue the other child's family along with the school. It's been a huge headache, but nothing that we don't deal with often.

Her cheeks tint just a touch at my question, and I can't help but bite my lip. Florence only flushes for three reasons I've noticed: a student destined for expulsion, the Texas heat, or a handsome man, like the contractors we've had in a few times. "Annabelle Teague's uncle wanted to discuss his niece with you. He was quite adamant about speaking with you immediately. I put him down for the soonest appointment available. Unfortunately, it meant cutting into that extra lunch break you were hoping for today."

"I need you to call him back and cancel it."

Her gaze widens, stunned at my reply. "Oh, dear, is everything all right?"

Releasing a heavy breath, I offer up a placating smile. "Of course, but I can't see him today."

"Would you like me to reschedule? I can look over your calendar; do you have a day in mind?" She begins to flip through the colorful planner in front of her next to her desktop computer. She has pictures of her kids and grandchildren filling the rest of the space along with a daisy. It looks suspiciously like the daisies that Annabelle Teague's uncle brought in with him. I threw my bouquet away after I kicked him out of my office.

"That's very kind of you, Florence, but I don't intend to ever speak to that infuriating man again if I can help it."

Her mouth drops open, flabbergasted at my blatant disdain for someone. I rarely show my displeasure to her or anyone else, for that matter, when it comes to dealing with students' parents or other family members.

She concedes, "Excuse me for pointing this out, but he doesn't strike me as the type to be pushed aside."

"You're completely right; he's ridiculously stubborn and obnoxiously demanding. I may have to call the police if he pushes me any further. I can't deal with someone like him, and I shouldn't have to on my lunch break either."

She quickly snaps a tissue from the box on her desk and dabs at her brow. "Well, I ah...I thought he was quite charming," she admits, blinking a bit too quickly.

"He's pushy, domineering, and rude," I scoff and gently lay my hand on her shoulder. I've upset the poor lady, and that wasn't my intention. Clearly, the vexatious male has Florence completely fooled, but not me. "I spoke to him already and trust me when I say he doesn't have anything that I need to nor want to hear."

"I'll give the young man a call back then and let him know you're indisposed. Shall I say the same if he doesn't answer, and he returns the message? We both know he's going to have something to say regardless," she assures me and sips from her lemon water.

"Yes, and that's much appreciated, Florence. Thank you."

She nods, and I carry on toward the conference room, straightening my suit jacket as I walk. I always attempt to appear the utmost professional; I oversee everyone in the building, after all. My freshly pressed blouse and slacks are just the small confidence boost I need to face my more pressing students and their parents. As a principal, I never look forward to this part of my job. Conferences with troublemakers usually tend to end up in a yelling match between an angry child and an embarrassed or stressed out parent. Having the proper attire when it goes down is critical to show them all that I mean business, and this matter is serious.

Jimmy Robertson's parents are due here any time now to discuss their son's repeated fighting. One more strike, and I'll be forced to expel this young man. I'm afraid he just isn't changing his ways, and there's only so much we can do for him here. Looking in at an elementary school, you'd never guess that fifth graders could cause any issues, but that's entirely untrue. Half of the boys are terrors. Testosterone starts to fill them at this age, and I find myself constantly fielding off their curiosity toward the girls and their ridiculous tempers toward other boys. This is just one of the many reasons why I refuse to have a child right now. I couldn't deal with it and these boys at the same time.

I should find an all-girls school and transfer. I could put my energy and expertise where it really matters. I'd say goodbye to obnoxious little boys as well as pushy bikers who think they run everything.

What kind of name is Blaze, anyhow? *So absurd.* I snort to myself and take a seat at the head of the conference table. That man has no idea who he's messing with. I may have given in to get him to leave, but I had to, or I was going to seriously lose myself, and he was not worth it. I won't let him gain the upper hand.

At least I don't have to worry about seeing him outside of after school dismissal. If he decides to be obnoxious, I'll just call the cops on him. We'll see if he really is friends with the sheriff or if he's fibbing. My guess is he's bluffing and would freak out if the police showed up. Maybe I'll see if they can stop by a few times this week just to shake the biker up.

Blaze

Flashing a wide smile at Florence, I lean in and place a soft peck on her hand. It works like a charm; she blushes, and her neck and cheeks flush. "Miss Florence, it's always a pleasure to see you, ma'am." I lure her in further with my politeness; older ladies can never resist it.

She waves her hand, and a bright smile lights up her face. "Oh, stop with the ma'am, young man!"

"Just being respectful." I grin, flashing my dimples and move a touch closer.

She grabs a tissue from the box on her desk and uses it to lightly pat the back of her neck. "You're such a charismatic fellow, I swear. I just don't see why Amelia wouldn't want to see you."

With a shrug, I play innocent, thinking back to her message regarding her boss. "I don't get it, either. I'm just looking out for my dear niece; without her momma around, she needs as many good people in her life as possible."

"Such a sweetheart," she murmurs quietly, and I don't know if she means Annabelle or me. It's a dick move throwing Torch's daughter into the mix, but he said I could. He'd rather me mention her a few times versus her having issues around here since she's a club brat.

"Miss Stone still thinks you were going to cancel my appointment, right?"

She nods and leans in, conspiring. "I was pretending that I couldn't get ahold of you with her, so if you showed up, it wasn't able to be helped. Amelia needs someone like you in her life. She doesn't realize it yet, but she will, in time."

Women like Florence always like to play matchmaker, and, in this case, it's worked to my advantage beautifully.

"Smart thinking." I wink, and she giggles a bit. "Now, you remember what we discussed?"

"Of course, and after this morning, I understand much more of what you were saying. She does need a short vacation—badly—bless her soul. That dear is so tightly wound up and won't take a moment to relax for herself. Take today, for example, she was willing to cancel her long lunch break to take on another meeting. Well, until she found out it was with you, that is."

"It's terrible." I sigh and shake my head. "She's going to work herself to death at this rate, then who would be here to help the students like she does?" I ask, and she pats my forearm, attempting to comfort me. I'm reeling her in like a gator with a bloody, raw chicken. Pretty sure I could get her to eat out of my palm if I tried.

"You're a good young man, willing to take her on a surprise vacation. I can't wait to see her come back in a few weeks after having good food, sunshine, and some sleep. The dear is thin as a rail."

"It's all that health junk she eats that you were telling me about," I agree, refraining from laughing.

One thing I've discovered about sweet Florence is she's a proud grandma to nine grandchildren. She's a true old-fashioned Southern lady who believes food, sweet tea, and sunshine is good for the soul. I do agree with her on that, and in this case, she thinks Amelia's putting her body through hell eating all the gluten-free, organic stuff she likes. I'd bet good money in Florence's house, macaroni and cheese is a staple, as is sweet tea, red meat, and watermelon—all my favorites. Anyhow, we had a long chat after I'd come in with Torch and again today over the phone.

"You're exactly what she needs."

"Thank you for that vote of confidence. I'll do my best. You canceled her other appointments?"

"Yes, they're all rescheduled for the week following her return. The less pressing meetings I've set up with the assistant principal to take in her place. I'll make sure it looks like she's here for the rest of the week to administration as well. She'll have a full two weeks of paid leave and won't have to lift a finger. It truly is the least we can do for all she does around here."

"You're a gem, Florence. I hope she appreciates you as much as you deserve."

She beams at the compliment and gestures for me to glance behind her. "That's the private entrance I was talking about when you called. Her car is parked in the first spot to the right of the door; you two can slip out there without any issues. Do you really think you can get her to go with you? She's a bit stubborn, I'm afraid."

It's too perfect; we'll sneak out the back door and drive her vehicle to the compound. It'll look like she's left on her own free will. Viking wanted me to bring a truck, but after speaking with Florence earlier, I've decided this would be the best plan. It'll have the least amount of possible blowback, and hopefully, no one will think anything suspicious of her departure.

"Yes, ma'am. You leave that part all up to me. We'll be quiet and not draw any unwanted attention either. In fact, I doubt you'll even hear us—maybe just the door opening and closing."

If Amelia even attempts to protest, I have just the thing to make her pass out right out. She'll be out like a light and damn near immediately. Luckily, we have a doctor on the payroll who was willing to help me out.

Her eyes light up as she stands. "Well, come on, let's get you tucked away in her office before she comes back. I don't want her putting that wall up and turning you away. She's a lucky woman. Back when I was her age, I'd have been beyond flattered to have a handsome fella like you coming to surprise me with a fancy trip all preplanned."

I wink at her again and round the counter to follow her back to Amelia's office. Florence is the only other one up here with the principal's key, so this part was imperative. The custodian doesn't even have a copy, because I was initially planning to go that route. Figured I could pay them off and take Amelia Stone by complete surprise.

Lucky for me, Florence is a romantic who I've convinced to be on my side. She thinks I want to take her high-strung boss on a surprise vacation and woo her. She'd probably faint if she knew I had something in my pocket to knock the bossy-ass woman out so I can kidnap her. I'm a bastard for deceiving Florence, but I've never claimed to be a good guy.

Before the Oath Keepers, I was what most would claim nightmares are made of. In the past, I'd never have hesitated to kidnap a woman for my old prez or even torture her. I'd tie her up and not think twice at my old brothers having their time with her. It was the way I was raised, so I didn't really grasp the consequences of how it affected the female. To me, it was just what the brothers did—what we did. We took what we wanted when we wanted it.

This time around was done with much more finesse and some patience. Viking should appreciate all the thought I've put into it, not going south. The club, along with Princess, has changed the way I treat women immensely. I've learned to spoil and protect them—the opposite of how I treated them before. I've quickly discovered that I don't have to take pussy from chicks. Most of them will quickly offer it up when they learn I'm even remotely interested. A little flirting and maybe a drink later, and those panties drop in no time.

Growing up under Joker—Viking and Odin's father as our club prez—he had all of us doing shit we'll forever regret. Evil twisted shit that'll haunt me for life. Not that any of it could've been helped.

Back then, we were doing what we had to, to survive. Joker would've killed us in a heartbeat had we faltered at his orders in any way. Thank fuck that's in the past, and Viking is nothing like his father was. The Oath Keepers never would've let us patch over. They hold a certain level of reverence amongst the clubs, and back when I was a Widow Maker, we never would've considered having morals.

"Good luck, Blaze," Florence wishes me and squeezes my bicep, drawing me away from my thoughts of the past. I step into the over-organized office, following her lead.

"Thank you," I mumble to the short woman, and she closes the door.

The first thing I do is head for the security feed and delete the entire week's footage for the front desk. Just in case someone does report Amelia Stone as missing, I need to cover my tracks and make it look like I was never here. She really is high strung and a control freak having the system in her office. Only two people have access to it, and that's just crazy when she has an entire school to keep an eye on.

Now, the real decision I have to make is, do I wait behind the door to surprise her? Or, should I sit my ass on her desk and witness the fury firsthand in her beautiful irises one last time before I use the knockout drug and take her with me? I know one thing for certain, I'm going to enjoy every moment of this.

My fingers rake over the dirty blond scruff on my jaw as I think of what would be best. Her fighting me would be much more fun, but she may make too much noise. I promised we'd be quiet. With a sigh, I step behind the door and eagerly await my woman's arrival. I've got a surprise for her—one she won't ever see coming or know how to stop.

Heathen

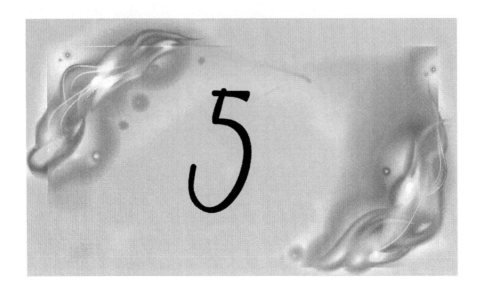

Amelia

My head's feeling heavy, my brain filled with grogginess. I'm consumed with an abnormal amount of fatigue. What on earth happened? Did I pass out? The last thing I remember was my meeting at school with Jimmy's parents. I'd finished discussing punishment options and walked back to my office. At least, I think I did. I don't remember ever making it to my desk, though. Ugh, I feel like I've been sick for a week, and I'm finally beginning to make my way out of it.

Inhaling, I roll over onto my stomach, noticing multiple things all at once. First of all, my wrists are squished together, my hands balled up into fists under my chest. This doesn't smell like my lavender vanilla detergent either, but rather, it's distinctly male.

I haven't had a man in my bed in God knows how long. That's not true; it's been two years since I'd invited anyone home with me. I blame it on a long day and too much wine, but even then, it was at a hotel and not my house. I was at a conference out of state...so a guy wasn't in my bed at home. Why on earth do I randomly smell one now?

The scent is a mixture of musky male, deodorant or cologne, and soap all meshed together. Inhaling again, my stomach tightens, and I groan, wanting to keep smelling it. Whatever dream I'm in, I don't want that part to end. I could cover myself in the scent and never get my fill. It's been too long since I've had sex. I've been busy and especially haven't wanted to deal with the potential of having a time-consuming relationship with anyone.

The air conditioner kicks on with a soft hum, and the sudden brisk breeze of cold air causes my nipples to stiffen. Now that isn't right. I must be dreaming because I don't ever sleep naked. I have a collection of comfortable satin nightgowns and flannel pajamas that I snuggle up in each night. I get a full chill, and my flesh covers in goosebumps. My body squirms, seeking warmth.

Where are all the blankets? Why's it so cold in here?

A big, rough palm lands on my bicep, and my body jerks in surprise as the warmth moves up and down, chasing the goosebumps on my arm. "Shhh," a deep, gruff voice coos quietly from behind, and my muscles tighten in response. My back's as stiff as a board, my frame constricting further as my mind finally clears up enough to grasp that I can't move my arms. I concentrate on the movement again but get nothing in return.

Don't freak out. It must be a dream, I chant, attempting to silently placate myself.

Everything is confusing and jumbled in my mind at the moment. I want to ask who's there and why in the hell I can barely move my body. I attempt to talk, even to cry out, but only a whimper manages to break free. *Why am I so damn groggy? What's wrong with me?*

"You're all right, babe. Just try and relax. It'll be easier coming out of the drugs if you don't fight. Slowly wake up and pull yourself out. You were unconscious for a while. You have to give your head some time to catch up with everything."

My eyes shoot open. There's no mistaking it; that was definitely a man. I'm exposed, naked, and vulnerable. *Was I in a wreck or something? I don't remember driving. Do I have amnesia? Why in the hell am I not wearing clothes?*

"Ugh," I manage as his palm moves to rub my back. I want to scream at him not to touch me, but I have to get my bearings first.

"Shh, babe," he soothes. I make myself refrain from jabbing my foot backward and telling him to shut up and not to call me babe. I'm not a pig. My name's Amelia Stone.

Glancing around, I take in the space. I'm nowhere that I recognize in the slightest. The room's pretty standard with off white walls and a charcoal, overstuffed chair. A five-drawer walnut finished dresser sits on the opposite wall; it's bare with only a flat-screen TV resting on top. There are two closed doors off to the side. If I'd have to guess, maybe it's a closet and a bathroom? The place is sparse, though—nothing to give away the location or who lives here. *Something had to have happened; I've never been here before.*

"W-where am I?" I ask after working my tongue around my mouth, and I clear my throat. I don't even sound like myself, my ears feel like I'm in a tunnel or something.

"You're in my room," he replies, and the voice registers. I know who that rich, gravelly, annoyingly sexy sound belongs to.

My eyes drop to my wrists as panic blooms in my chest. This can't be happening. I must be dreaming. I'm in denial; there's no way this can be real. Releasing a breath, I shift to my side, attempting to look at him. Maybe if I see him, I'll finally wake up—at least, I hope that's the case.

"Let me help, babe." He grabs onto my bicep again. I swallow my retort down as he pulls me to turn over, and I end up on my back.

The icy air hits my front, and I realize my mistake. I've presented my nakedness right out in the open. His determined, imperturbable cobalt gaze meets mine, and I gasp at finding him completely bare as well, lying beside me. His mouth turns up into his signature cocky smirk, and I scream bloody murder.

His grin drops, stricken by my sudden outburst, and then he's grabbing me. He yanks me to him, and in the next second, his lips are on mine. His moves bold and demanding, and I don't know how to react with everything hitting me all at once.

This isn't a dream; it's real. I'm naked and tied up in Blaze's bed. The truth hits me like a ton of bricks as I try not to lose myself in his demanding mouth. I've been kidnapped by the very man I was avoiding. He's trouble—a deceptively sexy criminal, and God help me, but I don't think he'll be letting me go anytime soon.

His scruff rubs my tender skin raw with the force he takes my lips with. It's consuming and utterly overwhelming. I've kissed my fair share of guys in the past, but none of them came at me with so much fervor. He's a man on a mission, and I'm normally in complete control. He's made me helpless and vulnerable to his will. His tongue caresses mine, and I manage to move my face enough to break away.

Panting, my glare meets his amused gaze. "Don't touch me!" I wail, taking in the feeling of his big, strong hands holding my biceps tightly in his clutches, his face in mine. *Omg, is he going to rape me?* Tears crest, and I plead, "Don't rape me! I'll press charges on you, you crude savage!"

His amusement drops, his features morphing to irritation. His coffee-scented breath coats my lips as he growls, "Shut up! I don't have to rape you to get what I want. Pussy isn't something I'm hurting for, so don't flatter yourself. Take that stick out of your uptight ass and think before you piss me off, and I decide to dump you in a ditch. Nature will be far crueler on you than I'm being right now."

"Whatever, just stay away from me, you heathen! Why are we naked?"

He shrugs, appearing not to have a care in the world. "Figured it was far past time to get your prissy ass out of those stuffy business clothes. As to why I'm naked? Simple. It's my bed."

"There's nothing wrong with my clothes, and I'd like them back right this instant. Also, untie me! This is kidnapping, and I won't hesitate to press charges. Men like you should be in jail."

His smile gleams. "First of all, I've been to jail, and it has nothing to offer, so I don't plan on returnin'. Second, I tossed your clothes in the trash the moment I got you out of them. I damn sure won't be getting you any others like them, so you're assed out. And third, you're right, this is kidnapping, so I won't be untying you. Whether you get free eventually or I kill you is entirely up to your behavior. We're surrounded by people who think like me, so don't even contemplate for a moment that anyone around here will help you outta this."

My lip trembles. I can't stop it no matter how hard I try, and it's beyond frustrating. This bullheaded man can't witness me being any more vulnerable than I already am at the moment. "I hate you," I eventually whisper because if my calming down will lead to my freedom, well, I'll do what I must. I've always been an intelligent person, and I won't stop being one now.

His mocking smile says it all. He doesn't have to tell me how my anger amuses him. I can see it written right in his expression. I've dealt with testy students and rude kids for years now; surely, I can deal with one cocky biker. This situation both terrifies and excites me. I've been drugged, taken, and held captive by a motorcycle-riding criminal. Yet, I'm here next to a naked man who has more muscles than the men's fitness magazine I saw last week in the supermarket. I must stay focused; it could be worse; I could be in the dingy, rat-infested meth lab I saw on the news yesterday. So far, this seems nothing of the sort, and thankfully, my law-breaking kidnapper seems to at least keep his living space clean.

"Good thing your words mean nothing—that *you* mean *nothing* to me." He sits up, propped on his elbow. He's got blond hair, bright blue eyes, dimples, scruff, and muscles galore.

I must memorize his appearance for when I eventually get free and contact the police. He's got a prominent nose and a scar under his left eye. It's not too noticeable unless you're looking for it. He's got another matching scar on the side of his nose and down his chin. Something happened to him, maybe a wreck or something to scar up that rough, almost pretty face of his. Even his lips pout, the thin scar splitting between his upper lip. The guy's so good-looking, no matter how much I want to pretend differently, that it makes me mad. Guys like him shouldn't get to look so enticing, especially when you know they're not up to any good.

"I'd let you take a picture," he remarks cockily, "but it wouldn't be good if you went to the cops with it." He sits up farther, his abs flexing. His member rests on his leg, and if it wasn't looking so comfortable, I'd swear he's hard with how big and thick he is. He flexes his hips, making his length jump, and my eyes fly up to his. Of course, they sparkle with amusement; he's thoroughly enjoying that he just caught me staring between his legs. My cheeks warm with embarrassment.

Rather than call me out on it, he moves, climbing out of bed. I'm left trying not to stare at him, yet wanting to so badly it's driving me crazy. *Will his butt flex as well? How can I think of that in a time like this?* "I'll lay it out right now, so I set your precious, scandalized mind at ease."

My gaze leaves the ceiling to find his again, and he continues, grabbing jeans from the floor. He works them over his hips. It's remarkable how something so simple as pulling on jeans can suddenly become so unbelievably sexy. Clearly, it's been too long since I've been with a man if I can look at my captor as I am. I should despise him, not think anything he does is remotely sexy or alluring. It's far too soon for me to be developing Stockholm Syndrome.

"Like I said earlier," he begins, "I don't need to take your pussy. In fact, I won't touch your pussy with my cock. You'll have to ask me for it to happen. Beg me even." He shrugs.

I immediately scoff. That'll never happen, no matter how much he may want it to. His brow rises, waiting. My lips slam closed, even though I have so many things I'd love to scream at him.

"You'll be here for a while. Don't try to escape because there are several people who will catch you and bring you right back. You eating, sleeping, showering—all of it—will be determined by your behavior. While you were knocked out, I had the doc remove that thing from your arm too."

My attention flies to my shoulder, and the small sting still present. "My birth control? You had my birth control removed?"

He nods. "It's gone. We did a sweep at your place, too, and disposed of all that hormonal shit you were taking to suppress your cycle. It may not happen overnight, but your estrogen and emotions will be given a chance to level back out."

"You have absolutely no right, whatsoever!"

"The hell I don't. I'm in control here, remember? That stuff, along with your skewed, irrational beliefs, has turned you into a snot nose bitch. I don't know who did a number on you back in the day to make you hate men, but that shit ends now. I don't care if you don't like me, that's your prerogative, but I'll be damned if you have that shit pumping through you to make you not think clearly."

"How does my birth control or my supplements have anything to do with that?" This man is delusional.

He taps the side of his head. "It messes with the chemicals up here."

Swallowing, I stare at him, transfixed. How can he know anything about the chemical structure in your brain and especially a woman's? Above all else, why's he doing this to me?

"I got to thinking when you didn't give in to my charm, not even a little, I had one of my brothers break into your spot when you were at work. He took pictures of everything, and I was able to see firsthand all the hormone suppressers and such you had. That's not normal for a woman to take; you're tricking your brain into thinking it doesn't need a man. You've been telling your body you don't need a man, but you're wrong. You need us to protect you and give you babies. It's been that way from the very beginning."

"I can do those things. I definitely don't need a man for any of them," I argue. He's ignorant to believe I need anyone for anything.

"No. A lab can give you a child, but that's not the way it's meant to be if you are able to have a child on your own. A gun could help protect you, but again, you're assed out, 'cause you're anti-gun. What's to protect you, say, if I broke in while you're sleeping? There's no way you can overpower me no matter what self-defense methods you may've Googled. You think a home alarm will protect you from me?"

He shakes his head, continuing and making me question everything I've believed. "It won't for about six and a half to ten minutes while the signal is transmitted, they try calling you and finally dispatch the police—who, if you're lucky, aren't already busy helping with some catastrophe going on. You think you could fight someone like me off you for ten minutes? You wouldn't last for thirty seconds with me, but if I was beside you, to protect you? I'd decapitate the motherfucker who attempted to touch my woman."

I swallow, turned on and furious. "I could have a child without a man in a lab, as you've pointed out."

"Right now, you may be able to, but what if the labs go away? Then what?"

"But they won't," I argue. "I don't need a man; I never will."

"You're wrong. Regardless, this is the position you're in. You're at my mercy, and no matter how strong you may think you are, I'm in control. If you want this situation to be easier on you, then I suggest you get on board and learn to keep your rude remarks and names to yourself."

"This subject isn't over," I say stubbornly, wanting to prove my point that I don't—and won't ever—need a man.

"On that, you're right, but I'm done talking about it for the time being. Now that you know the score, I'll give you some time to process." He finishes pulling on his boots then leaves, closing the door behind him without another glance in my direction.

I don't have any idea of what to think about everything we just talked about. The only thing I can come up with is that this man is completely crazy. Out of all the guys, I had to come across the delusional one. Not only that, but he has me bound and naked and completely at his mercy. I have to figure a way out of here. There's no way I can let this crazy man have his way with me.

Blaze

I rake my hands through my hair and exhale. This woman has me twisted up inside in some type of way. My ass has been planted on this uncomfortably hard bar stool since I left my room and her behind in it.

"You all right, cousin?" Odin asks, sliding onto the seat beside me. He's my MC brother but also my cousin by blood.

Glancing over at him, I sigh, frustrated, and admit, "I don't think so."

His brow wrinkles, not sure what to make of my answer. He gestures to Frost to serve us a round of drinks. "What's up?"

"I got the principal. And by got her, I mean literally. The bitch is tied up and all."

He nods. "That's good, right?"

I shrug. "Yes and no. Spider went in and photographed everything for me. He pointed out to me all the stuff she's been taking to suppress her menstrual cycle along with some other feminist propaganda bullshit hating on men. Not the good woman-supporting-woman type, but the kind who bashes any male with half an opinion that disagrees with her. This is bad...worse than what I was expecting when it came to her. I'll be real with you; I'm not too sure what I'm doing with her."

His eyes widen at my words. He exhales a discouraged sigh and says, "Wow. I knew she was a tough one, but it sounds like you may have your hands full with this chick." He frowns deeply, mimicking the way I'm feeling as well.

"She's infuriating," I admit, frustrated. "She truly believes that she doesn't need men for anything, not even protection. The female is delusional."

"I thought this was about getting her away from the school so the kids would stop having issues with her. Are you trying to get her to see reason or somethin' else?"

"It was, initially," I concur. "But when I saw all those photos and everything Spider laid out for me, it began to make sense why she hates me so much and why she's not into me at all."

"Is that what this really is? You're upset she doesn't like you? Since when have you cared what anyone has thought about you, especially an uppity bitch?"

I shrug again, my hands yanking at my blond locks. Frost sets a couple new beers in front of us, along with a bottle of whiskey and shot glasses, sensing the heaviness of Odin's and my conversation. "I don't give a shit, normally. With her, however, it's driving me fuckin' crazy, because she's got it all wrong. She believes me and other men like me are the enemy when that's not the case at all. She doesn't understand we're protectors; if anything, we're a woman's biggest asset."

He whistles between his teeth. "Damn, bro. She's really gotten to you. I'm not much with woman advice. Cherry was easy on me where that's concerned. Once I finally opened my eyes and pulled my head outta my ass, she was already waiting for me. Have you spoken to Princess about it? She's better with this sorta shit."

I shake my head. He's probably right, though. Princess knows everything, it seems. I thought she was a prissy barbie doll bitch when I first caught wind of her, but I can easily understand why Viking is so taken with her and put a ring on her finger. The ice princess is a bad bitch once she thaws toward you.

"Give it a shot...she might be able to help you."

"If she doesn't skin my ass for kidnapping the woman."

He snickers. "Typically, I'd tell you to run for the hills, but this is club business. P knows not to meddle in that shit. She's aware of where she stands when it comes to Oath Keepers shit."

"Bet," I agree and take a swig from the bottle. The crisp cold beverage goes down smoothly; it was just what I needed at the moment. Along with my cousin's company and his advice, I'm not feeling quite as conflicted anymore. Sure, I'm torn up inside about it all, but at least I have some sort of plan of action in place now.

"Vike know you have the principal already?"

"Yeah, the bitch is tied up in my room right now, so I sorta had to tell him."

He chuckles. "No wonder she's got you pegged as enemy number one. I bet she's as pissed as a cat in water."

"You have no fucking idea, bro."

"Definitely call P. Maybe even have her go in and torment the chick a bit for good measure. It'll take the focus off you so much. The principal will have to deal with a real boss bitch. She may even get her feelings hurt."

"True. She actually believes she's smarter than me. She may be more intelligent book-wise, but she has no idea about street smarts. The woman is clueless. I had to break it down Barney style just to get her to see how irrational her belief is on being safe by herself versus if she had me at her side."

"Oh, I bet she just loved that."

Releasing a breath, I shake my head. "You have no idea. This female may be the death of me yet."

"You've survived the Iron Fists and damn near bleeding out; you can get through one strong-minded chick."

"Oh, I have no doubt. I'm just wondering if I'll bash my head against the wall trying to get her to see reason in the process."

He snickers again, and I grumble. The woman is so stubborn, and she called me a *heathen*. Who says that shit to someone else? Her, apparently...but still, she's something else. Maybe Princess can talk some sense into her, though I won't hold my breath on it.

"Called me a *heathen*," I murmur with a furious hiss, and he busts up. "Shut up, dickmunch."

"I never thought it'd happen—that there'd be a chick not susceptible to your charm. Eh, *Casanova*, it could be worse."

My brow raises, and I give him a *get the fuck outta here* look.

"Hey, all women could think you're a heathen, instead of only one." He shrugs like it makes total sense, and I scowl. "There's always Honey, brother. She can never get her fill of you."

"True," I concede, grouchy over this entire conversation, or maybe just in general. "I think I'll have P go talk or maybe even knock some sense into the uppity bitch while Honey sucks my cock."

"Sounds like win-win to me, Blaze."

I nod, feeling better already. Just the thought of my cock in a sexy female's mouth gets me excited. But not just any woman. I want it stuffed between ol' principal's lips while she hums in pleasure. Now that's one hell of a thought.

"Have you seen Vike's woman around, or is she at the house?" I pour a shot of whiskey and throw it back. I usually know where Princess is more than anyone else here, aside from her ol' man, but I've been preoccupied with my own shit today.

"Last I saw she was headed for Viking's office."

"I'll finish my beer then. They're probably fuckin'."

"Definitely fucking," he agrees and takes a swig of his beer.

Mercenary and Chaos join us. Merc sits next to Odin and Chaos next to me. "Brothers," we greet one another.

"What's up?" I ask no one in particular.

"Not much," Chaos replies while Mercenary orders something from Frost and bitches that he wants French fries. "You good, brother?" he asks.

"I'm straight, just needing to speak with P. Heard she's in the office with her ol' man, though, and don't want to interrupt that meeting."

He nods. "I get it. I just saw them, though, and they still had all their clothes on," he chuckles, signaling for a beer.

"In that case, I'm going to go catch them before it changes, and they're tucked away for a hefty part of the day."

"Probably a good idea," he agrees.

I say my goodbyes, making my way to our prez's office.

The door's wide open, and I find Princess sitting on her ol' man's lap. Thankfully they aren't going at it. Not that I haven't seen it in the past, I just need to speak to her. "Hey." I poke my head in the door and lightly rap on the thick barrier.

Vike chin-lifts, inviting me inside. "Brother?" he asks as I plop down on the couch and make myself comfortable.

"I needed your wife's advice if you don't mind."

"Ah." He lovingly smacks her thigh, making her grin.

P pecks a kiss to his cheek. "How about you go eat a piece of that cake before it's all gone and you're left pouting until I bake another? There's also fried chicken from last night."

"I don't pout," he grumbles like an embarrassed kid.

She smiles. "Of course not. I was in the kitchen earlier, and there were only two slices left."

"Fine." He exhales the word and moves to stand. He mumbles, "Don't see why you can't just leave it at home anyway."

"'Cause, you'll eat it all and then complain about not getting enough gym time."

Viking gives her a look but doesn't argue. He knows she's got his ass pegged. He presses a kiss to her forehead and fist bumps me on his way out. His desk is massive, making Princess appear tiny sitting behind it. With my fam' no longer distracting his wife, I make myself more comfortable by stuffing pillows behind me and dive in, telling her everything.

Once my cock has been sated, and I can finally relax a bit, I head back to my room. I never came back to check on my mouthy captive, although it was probably for the best. We both needed some time to stew in our thoughts and chill out. I gave her a hefty dose of some mixed-up doping cocktail from the doc, so she most likely dozed off and on for the remainder of the day. Those types of drugs always make people drowsy and nauseous. I could maybe chalk that up to her motherfuckin' heathen comment, but something inside me says she'd call me that no matter what.

I'm quiet when I enter the now dark area. Only my bathroom light remains on. I should've checked in on her to see if she at least needed a restroom break. In the past, when I've kidnapped chicks, I'd never offered them anything. I'd just locked them up in a dog cage and let Joker do what he pleased with 'em. He'd eventually have his fill and pass them on to the remaining members who were interested in having their turn.

I'm determined to do it differently this time around. I won't put her in a cage unless she becomes too much to handle. I seriously doubt that will happen, although she's got a mouth on her, but she's not unruly physically. I'm not going to fuck her unless she asks me for it, either. I refuse to have that on my conscious, and besides, it'd just feed into her misconstrued notions on all white men being the devil. This shit being plastered across social media recently that men are the enemy is ridiculous. After seeing what she had in her house and on her devices, she clearly believes some of that crazy horseshit.

Peeling my clothes off, I slide into bed next to her warm, motionless frame. She's sleeping soundly. Wouldn't surprise me if she needed the drugs just so she could get some decent sleep like this. She seems to have the stick so far up her ass that it'd make her sleep-deprived and feed into her bitchiness.

Hauling the down comforter over us, I lay next to her, naked and restless. I had my cock sucked earlier, and I thought it'd sated me, but being this close to Amelia has my body saying otherwise. She's far too perfect looking to be tucked into my bed without any of her clothes on. I'll have to grit through it though, cause she's not getting them back. Ever. The suit was hot, but she used it as a tool—like a mask—to help her keep up that "too good" persona. Leaving her naked and exposed keeps her vulnerable and me in control that much more.

With the shit she's already said, the least I deserve is something sexy to look at in the process. I told ol' Florence that I'd keep Amelia away for about two weeks on vacation, but who knows when I'll really let her go back. It all depends on her and how long she holds out on this built-up animosity toward men and her despising bikers attitude. If I can get her on our side, then I'll let her loose sooner than later. If not...well, I hate to see what becomes of her if she attempts to cause any more issues for the club. The MC doesn't condone violence against women, but a problem is a problem, and she'll disappear somehow. I'm sure it'll be by my hand too; I'm good at cleaning up messes.

With that thought, my eyes close, and I drift off, exhausted from a hard day's work.

Amelia

I'm lying in Blaze's bed, having attempted to get my ties loose. I've failed miserably so far. It's hard doing anything without wiggling and shaking the bed too much. I figured now was my best chance. Who knows what Blaze has in store for me once he wakes up. I'm finally awake enough to concentrate, having slept many hours yesterday and last night. I can't remember the last time I've had so much rest, probably sometime before I went off to college. I struggled with my restraints yesterday, eager to get free, but it was a lost cause. I was too out of it to get anywhere with anything.

So here I am, jerking and biting at the rope that's tightly wound around my wrists. Each time Blaze's soft snoring pauses, my body tenses, hoping he remains asleep. It's frustrating and painful as the coarse threads dig into my sensitive skin. They're no longer pink, but an angry, raw red. Blood's gathered, peppering my skin, just waiting for me to rub against it once more to release the droplets. I'd like to believe this day couldn't get any worse, but that would be foolish. I'm assuming I'm in a motorcycle club facility of some sort, though Blaze hasn't admitted as much. With that in mind, anything could happen to me.

Maybe getting free isn't a good idea, as I don't know what's waiting for me outside this room. It's a chance I must take, though, fearing they may want to kill me at some point. Though, if I try to be rational about it and believe him, he claimed yesterday that my treatment is up to my behavior. If they wanted me dead, wouldn't I already be that way? And he told me he wouldn't force himself on me. So far, he's held true to that as well. It's hard for me to trust anything he says, though. His actions, in the end, will determine that, I suppose.

I don't understand it. Why would he kidnap me? I don't have a lot of money in my bank account, and my parents aren't wealthy. I'm not worth much to anyone. It doesn't make sense. If I can't break free of these wrist ties, I'm going to ask him exactly that when he wakes up. I'd turned on my side away from him, but not before I'd gotten an eyeful of his bare chest. And what a chest; geez, the man must be carved from stone or something.

I can't believe I'm even going there; the guy kidnapped me. I refuse to fall victim to Stockholm Syndrome. Besides, he's an infuriating big-headed bastard.

He shifts, moving the bed with him, and then I'm weighed down by a massive arm. I say that because his bicep is like three of mine put together. No wonder the uncouth beast is so sure of himself when it comes to fighting someone off. However, that fact doesn't mean I'd ever admit it to him. The last thing he needs is for me to say he's right about anything.

Blaze's arm is warm with its resting weight, and when he turns into me more, he heats my exposed back as well. The appendage rests there for a moment before he's using it to turn my body toward him. I was hoping this wouldn't happen, that he'd interrupt me from getting my binding free. Holding my breath, I can't help but peek at his face, trying to gauge how much his sleeping has been disturbed. He's silent, his breaths coming a bit quicker than before. In this position, I can't help but inhale deeply and catch his manly scent. If the circumstances were any different, I'd revel in the smell, but not here, nor now.

With a drowsy grumble, he murmurs, "Tuck into my chest; you'll be warmer that way."

He wants me closer? Does he even know what he's telling me right now? This guy is ridiculously confusing.

At first, I'm completely still. I want him to go back to sleep as quickly as possible to leave me to my plans. After a moment of my noncompliance, his big paw wraps more securely around my back, bringing me closer to his form. The realization hits me that we're both completely naked in his bed. I won't let him worm his way into having sex with me, and by the thick appendage pressed against my leg, he clearly enjoys morning sex. I have to get away. I won't allow him to have me without a fight.

I begin to squirm, doing whatever I can to attempt to work my way out of his grip and away from his sinfully tempting bulk. Warm body or not, I won't openly allow him to touch me—ever. He's taken far too many liberties as it is witnessing me naked, kidnapping me and barking at me as if I'm his property to do with as he pleases. The man has nerve like no other.

My jiggling around stirs him further, and his lids slowly part, his baby blues meeting my own terrified gaze. I panic, trying to come up with something to say to distract him from what I was attempting to do. I don't want him to find out I was trying to escape and freak out on me or kill me for disobeying him.

"What are you doing?" I manage to choke out, light-headed from holding my breath and chewing on the rope. My teeth hurt, and I think the rope scratched my tongue.

He's grabbing for me, then holding me to him in his strong grip. Some may find enjoyment being held by a big man, but not me. The move only frightens me even more than I already am. *Will this be the day he forces himself on me?*

His azure irises take in my face and my unwelcoming expression. He clears his throat and gruffly admits, "You were shaking." His shoulders bounce. "Your skin's cold. I was keeping you warm." He says it so bluntly that I almost believe that he didn't have an ulterior motive. This is a man, though; of course, he has a motive. At this point, I wouldn't put anything past him. I underestimated him before, and I can't afford to make that mistake twice.

"I was shaking because you kidnapped me!" I huff, peeved at his simple explanation. "I'm cold because you keep the air conditioning ridiculously low in here, and you've taken my clothes from me. I was stuck in here all day yesterday without so much as a blanket...of course, I'm cold!" I glare as fiercely as I can manage, but I doubt it intimidates him. Blaze is like a boulder—unflinching and steadfast.

"I covered you up when I came to bed," he fires back, peering at me like *I'm* the crazy one. It only fuels my irritation, making me fume inside at his irrational reasoning. I doubt he thinks he's done anything wrong at all by kidnapping me since he thought to cover me up. I scoff, and his expression turns stern.

"How does that help me all day yesterday? I've been chilled since then. At this rate, I may catch hypothermia. So much for not hurting me."

He scowls. "You're being overly dramatic. Besides, coming down off strong drugs, you're usually hot or cold and sweat a lot. I figured you'd be hot and sweaty and want the air and space to detox." He shrugs. "How was I supposed to know you'd be the opposite?"

"Oh my God," I murmur, completely outraged. *This guy's unbelievable.* "Perhaps you'd have known if you'd thought to come and check on me? What if I had to use the bathroom? What if I'd been attacked?"

His brow raises. "I didn't hear any screaming; figured you were fine. I wasn't coming in here yesterday until you'd calmed the fuck down and stopped acting like an entitled bitch."

His words make something inside me snap. In the next second, I lean forward and bite his chin. I clamp down, wanting to inflict as much damage as possible. I don't use profanity, but *fuck him and the horse he rode in on.*

"What the ever-lovin' fuck!" he shouts, jerking back. His hand comes to my face and squeezes my chin and cheeks so hard it brings tears to my eyes, and I release my bite. He gives my face another tight squeeze and flings my head back. I rocket backward with the momentum, and it feels like my neck snaps. "That kind of shit will get you fucked up real quick. You feel me? You hurt me, bitch, and I'll fuck you up." His hands ball into fists, and he lets out a terrifying growl. I don't doubt for a second that he could harm me badly.

Tears stream down my face. I'd done my best yesterday not to let him see me like this, but his hold hurt. I've never been a violent person, and harming someone or being injured isn't fun to me. "Don't touch me!" I manage to brokenly whisper as tears continue to spill freely.

His forehead scrunches, and his jaw flexes as he grits his teeth. "You moved first; remember that, Miss Fucking Perfect."

"But I'm a woman a-and you put your hands on me."

He snorts and rolls his eyes. "Now you want to pull the female card? Let me clue you in. You wanna be treated like a woman? Fuckin' act like one. You wanna fuck with me? I'll fuck back. You're pulling your shit with the wrong type of man, babe."

I sniff, my tears still falling over my heated cheeks. I bet my nose is bright red and swollen. It always gets like that when I'm upset. I could never hide it well when I cried, and he's learning it firsthand that I'm easy to read when I'm not in one of my pressed suits behind the counter at work. I don't have those layers of protection to help me stand apart. I glance down, and it's the wrong move because he follows my gaze.

"Ah, shit, babe, what'd you do?" He reaches to pull my wrists out towards him so he can get a better look.

I shrug and quietly confess, "I wanted to get them off." The blood's risen to the top of my skin, peppering the pale flesh with dots. My struggle moments ago seems to have been the last straw for the area that's been closely wrapped with rough rope, as droplets of blood run over my arms and underneath.

"Damn it, you hurt yourself. If you'd kept that up, you'd have given yourself scars. The ties would've hurt you more, too, and wouldn't allow those cuts to heal properly. You're so stubborn...wish you'd just listen to me," he says with a perturbed exhale.

My teary gaze meets his, and I find myself biting my lip as he reaches up, drying my tears away with his fingers. "Why do you even care?" I ask, not complaining or shying away from his hands.

His expression softens, "Because, believe it or not, I've always been the one to take care of the women. Whether it was kidnapping them and locking them up or else fighting to protect them so much that it nearly kills me. One way or the other, I've always been the one responsible for 'em. You need to decide which one you want me to be when it comes to you. The man that cages the bird or cares for it."

I swallow, quiet, unsure of what to say. My stare remains glued to him as he climbs out of bed and heads for the bathroom. My eyes betray me, stealing a glance at his tantalizing behind. I'm still staring in the same spot when he returns, and I'm rewarded with a quick peek at his member. Of course, his shaft is big; I'd expect nothing less. when it comes to someone as cocky as he is. He has a great butt and an impressive member. It makes me hate him a little more, I think.

He returns with a decent sized first aid kit and sits on the bed directly beside me. He opens the white box and reaches for my hands. His length lies against his leg—imposing, but not completely hard. I want to stare so badly, but I wouldn't dare allow it. How can he be so brazen with his nakedness? He acts like this is completely normal to just walk around naked and be in front of whoever. Maybe for him, it is. I mean, I do it at home, but I'm alone there.

"Why are you helping me?" I ask. I watch him, curious to see if he knows what he's doing.

He's silent as he works. He unwinds gauze, rubs my skin with a few alcohol pads, and pats it dry with the sterile gauze. Once he's satisfied with cleaning it and wiping the blood away, he applies ointment and then wraps my wounds with more of the gauze. He tears a strip of medical tape using his teeth and utilizes the contaminated tape to secure the bandage on each wrist. Once he has them how he wants, he moves my bindings farther down my arm, so they're positioned underneath the gauze wraps.

He eventually meets my inquisitive gaze and answers, "Because, regardless of what you may believe, I don't want you to be in any sort of pain."

I bite the inside of my cheek, unsure of what else to say.

"Do you need the bathroom?" He changes the subject, and I'm grateful for it.

"Yes." Anything to get me out of this bed and allow me to scout around another area.

He stands, and then I'm being hauled up into his strong arms. I squeal, completely out of my element and caught off guard at how he easily manhandles me yet is careful enough to not bump my injured wrists. "Whoa! What do you think you're doing?"

"You need the bathroom, but your legs are tied. I'm taking you to the toilet."

"I am not peeing in front of you!"

"Relax, your highness; you can manage without me watching you. I'm leaving the door open, though, so don't get your hopes up too high."

He needn't worry about it. My hopes aren't high right now, about him or anything else.

The day passes excruciatingly slowly. Blaze does come back to check on me, though. He takes me to the bathroom again and gives me a big plate of macaroni and cheese with sweet tea to drink. When I ask for a salad, he just laughs at me and leaves the room. He doesn't seem to be too concerned with me having a plastic spoon or straw. I'm no jailbird, though, so it's not like I know how to make a shank out of it anyway. I can only be stubborn for so long before my stomach decides to growl ridiculously loud, and I give in. Cold macaroni and cheese at this point is the best thing I can remember eating in who knows how long. I don't usually have much sugar if I can help it, but I was so thirsty, I sucked down the tea as soon as he put it in my hands.

"Can I have clothes?" I probe the next time he comes back to the room.

He rolls his eyes and snorts. "Maybe in a week. Maybe never, it depends on you."

A gasp escapes as my mouth falls open. "A-a week? But my job...people will know I'm gone. They'll look for me."

He shakes his head and offers me a smirk. "Nah, I got it all covered. Sorry to break it to you, babe, but no one will be worrying about you for some time."

"What? How is that even possible? You realize I'm the principal of an entire school, right? That comes with meetings, paperwork, responsibilities. You're going to get me fired from my job if you called in or whatever for me. Besides, that's not like me. They'll eventually catch on; everyone knows I'm unmarried."

He flashes a bit of teeth with his smug expression. "As far as they're concerned, you're on vacation. From what I gathered, you have plenty of days saved up. I have more than enough time with you to make you completely disappear if I wanted to."

I'm flabbergasted. How could he have any idea about my personal work affairs? I have over thirty days saved up. What can I say? I'm a workaholic and try not to take any days off unless it's necessary. My unspent vacation time from my previous school position spilled over into this job, so they've been accumulating for years now. They were eager to accept my request to have them carry over. It meant me coming to work immediately versus them having to wait even longer without a principal. They were practically desperate to fill the position, so I was able to negotiate some.

"I don't understand. I have to put in special paperwork to take anything over a few days off. They have to find someone to temporarily come in to help or else shift my schedule to the assistant principal and such." I probably shouldn't tell him any of this, but hopefully, it'll make him think twice.

Blaze divulges, "I know all that already. It's taken care of, babe. So, get used to the fact that no one is searching for you now and they won't be. Hell, no one cares." He shrugs with his cutting remark, and I try to choke the tears away that are threatening to surface. He has my emotions all over the place, and I feel like I'm losing it.

I've never felt more vulnerable in my life. I'm normally strong and independent, but this man won't even allow me to walk to the bathroom. He carries me each time I need to move; he plates up my food and cleans up after me. It's demeaning, let alone the huge fact that he's kept me naked for the past two days as well.

He'd bandaged me up this morning as I'd tried to escape, and he was, dare I say it...his actions were caring the way he'd doctored my wounds. Afterward, I felt like I'd been acting childish, rubbing my wrists raw to escape. It's all futile, he seems to have it figured out, and it's obviously not his first kidnapping. I'm beginning to believe him about his experience with doing it plenty of times before. The thought terrifies me because what happened to all the other women he'd nabbed?

The tears I'd been trying so hard to keep locked away trail over my cheeks once again. I've lost count at this point how many times I've allowed myself to cry. My nose will tattle on me soon as well by turning bright red. I can never hide my crying.

He leans in, lightly rubbing my tears. His forehead scrunches. Under different circumstances, I'd almost think he was cute like this. He doesn't seem to understand why I'm crying, and it clearly concerns him. Could he truly be some sort of heathen kidnapper biker who cares if I cry? That wouldn't make any sense at all.

"What happened to them?" I whisper, and his expression falls flat, locking into a solemn frown.

Blaze stands to his full height, hands on his hips. He's an intimidating man, I won't deny that much. "You don't want to know," he says after a beat of tense silence. "Even more of an incentive for you to behave."

"But what if I do everything you want, and you still...kill me?" I whisper, not wanting to utter the words. "Shouldn't I...uh, fight and attempt everything I can to get away? To get help?"

I expect him to chuckle, but he remains somber. "You hear of those stories with kidnap victims miraculously escaping and finding help. I've seen them too. I know what you're thinking right now. But, babe, it won't happen for you. Let me lay it out for you a bit. Say you do get out of my room somehow; there's an entire clubhouse full of my brothers waiting on the other side of that door." He gestures to the door on the far wall. "Some of them are a lot worse than me. Take Annabelle's father, for example, he wouldn't hesitate to bury you, especially since you've been fucking with his daughter. You really want him to see you running free in the hallway? Let's say you manage to make it outside the clubhouse...you know what's surrounding it?"

I shake my head. I have no idea. I've done my best to stay away from this place and them. I've heard whispers around town of the local biker club. I've seen various guys in their leather vests in the stores and riding around. I've always kept my distance in those cases.

"Well, there's a tall ass fence that's wrapped with barbed wire and has electricity running through it. The electrical current will either put you out or kill you since your frame's so thin. There are cameras everywhere outside, and there's also my brothers guarding the gate and doing their patrols. We're a big club with lots of shit to protect. You won't be leaving here unless I walk your ass out, take you back to that school, and decide to let you go. You're a little caged bird...and babe, I'm the only one with your key."

I swallow, biting my lip as reality sets in, and then the tears hit me hard—much harder than before. Sobs wrack my body, turning me into a complete mess, but none of that matters. What does matter is everything he's just shared with me, the truth of his words that I can't get free no matter how hard I try to.

"Crying won't do you any good, sugar. It's time you face your circumstances. You behave the way you ought to, and you may make it out of this alive and unharmed."

I exhale and nod, trying to get my tears to stop. He's right. I need to pull myself together and get through this. I'm a strong woman. If anyone can survive being kidnapped from a biker club, it's me. Now, doing it without attempting to bite him again, that's another thing entirely. This man is controlling, pigheaded, and infuriating.

At my nod of submission, he goes to the closet and removes the thick down comforter from the high shelf and brings it back to the bed. He covers me, tucking the warmth around me and murmurs, "I'll be back later."

I nod again and wiggle until I'm turned onto my side. My body aches from lying in the bed for two days straight, but at least he's finally covered me up. Laying in this room naked all day has me seriously feeling like I'm freezing.

It's past time I come to terms with my current circumstances, I could be much worse off than I am right now. He could be beating, raping, and starving me or who knows what. He's done none of those things, and tonight, I'm finding a reason to be thankful. Blaze wants me naked and compliant to him? Fine, but I won't offer myself up to him sexually. I'll be accommodating with personal respect for myself. Most of all, I'll stay alive. Damn it, I have to, no matter what.

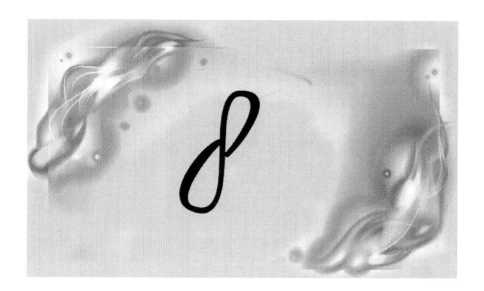

Blaze

"How's it goin, brother?" Torch questions with a grumble as I take my spot in church. Viking's not in here yet, it's just me, Torch, and Smokey. Those two are always here first; I guess the secretary and death dealer are more responsible than the rest of us.

I toss Smokey my club dues and shrug at Torch. I throw back my tumbler that's half full of Jack, and the liquid doesn't burn enough. Not like it used to. "She started crying last night," I quietly share, not caring for the way it makes me feel saying it aloud.

His brows jump, and he emits a low whistle between his teeth. His canines look sharp as fuck. The motherfucker reminds me of some kind of vampire or some shit when he shows his teeth. "Making progress already?"

"Hard to tell," I say, moving my gaze around the quiet room and empty chairs. "Only a few days in. Plus, she's off all that shit she'd been putting in her body. The doc said it could make her moody and emotional. I figure she'll be here long enough to detox off it all and maybe come back down to fuckin' reality."

He shakes his head, flabbergasted. "Hard to believe a woman that book smart would want to do that to her body."

"Bro, it's the fake media feeding these women all this bullshit that we're trying to take over the world. They need to come to terms that we took that shit over way back, but there have been plenty of women in charge too. Shit, most of the powerful men in the world have a strong woman right beside them. The news is so concerned with twisting us to look like evil villains, they leave off the part about us coveting our women." I sigh, disgruntled. "They forget to mention that we try to help women succeed, too, and we don't think they're below us."

"Glad I don't have to deal with that shit. Annabelle won't grow up believing any of that bullshit. She'll see firsthand what real men are," he grumbles.

"When's Flame get out of the pen?" His baby momma has been locked up for years. He doesn't speak about her to any of us, but I know he keeps tabs. He has to for Annabelle's sake. If Flame ever got out, she'd want her daughter back; of that, I have no doubt.

"Last I heard, not anytime soon. She keeps getting more time added on...you know how she is."

"She finds out you're here, she'll come for her daughter."

He shrugs. "Won't be the first time I dealt with the crazy bitch."

"Crazy is putting it lightly; she's on another level."

His lips turn up. He knows I'm right. Though with Torch's mean ass, it's only expected he'd end up stuck with the wildest chick out of everyone. He tried to cut ties when she got locked away, but Flame won't let him off that easy. She gets out, and she'll be on a warpath once she discovers he and Annabelle aren't still in the Carolinas.

The door swings open and we're interrupted by several brothers. They nod their hellos and toss money at Smokey for their club dues. Viking takes his place at the head of the table and waits for a few beats until everyone's inside and seated before he hits the gavel to call church in session.

"Lotta shit to get through today," he barks, cracking his knuckles.

We echo with our own grumbles, not fond of being brought into church so damn early. We usually do this shit later in the day after we've had a chance to sleep off part of our hangovers.

He carries on. "I've been in touch with the Nomads. Spider tells me that border patrol is struggling. With more illegals crossing by the day, it's too much for them to fight with the cartel as well. They're getting hit from all directions. ICE has been doing raids on the down low, and from what I hear, the government is dispatching soldiers down south. Everything is being kept quiet, out of the mainstream media, to avoid a press shitshow that seems to be happening constantly. Luckily, Exterminator still has undercover connections; otherwise, we'd be fucked as far as this intel goes."

Nightmare lightly raps his knuckles against the table and asks, "So what's the plan? What are we going to do about it?"

"Normally, I'd recommend that we keep our noses the fuck outta it. Those cartel fuckers know Texas is Oath Keepers' turf. We have the largest MC presence in the state. They'll be expecting the Nomads, but they won't be expecting two clubs riding. I've spoken to Ares. It's time we pony up and show them we don't take kindly to their unauthorized distribution and murders in our state. The sex trade is bad enough, but they start throwing in the other shit, and we have to put a stop to it. Give them the boot."

"'Bout motherfuckin' time," Night growls, and Saint starts twitching with excitement. He's been cooped up for too long; the brother needs some crazy in his life.

"Torch will man the club. Smokey, you'll stay back with him. We'll lock down the compound, but also make sure all your ol' ladies are strapped. Take them out shooting tonight to get them practicing and brushing up on their aims. Ares's chapter is doing the same. They're loading the ol' ladies up with plenty of ammo and telling them to shoot first and ask questions later."

Sinner chin-lifts, garnering our attention. He shakes his head. "We've tried to teach Jude. She's good with a knife, but she's not confident with a Glock."

Chaos nods. "She's a sweetheart. Have the girls keep her busy with Maverick and making food. Her help in those things will keep the others focused. If Princess isn't distracted, she's as fierce as one of us staying back."

Nightmare interrupts. "Same. After the Iron Fists, Bethany has been on the warpath. She's been kickboxing and visiting the range weekly. She won't be a victim again."

Mercenary speaks up. "Chevelle's a bad bitch; she'll hold her own. If she has to, she'll run a fucker over."

Viking smirks. "Not a doubt in my mind that they can't hold the fort down with Torch and Smokey around to help. The Iron Fists caught us off guard and fucked us up...we learned our lesson the hard way."

"Fuckin' Fists," Nightmare growls, and Viking raises his hands to get everyone to shut the hell up.

"We're getting off topic. We'll ride out in three or four days; it depends on what updates I receive. Be prepared to pop smoke any day."

Clearing my throat, I bring up a sore spot for me. "I have the principal in my room...tied up still."

Viking's brow raises as he trains a stony expression on me. "And? You haven't broken her yet?"

I shake my head. "I thought kidnapping her would shake her up enough to get her to roll over and comply, but she's stubborn. Caught her chewing at her wrist ties yesterday. Bloodied up her arms and everything. She's stubborn."

Torch divulges, "She called him a heathen."

Several brothers around the table break out in chuckles, and I have to grit my teeth as to not growl in return.

Viking exhales, quickly running out of patience. "You have four days, Blaze. Turn up the heat and fucking break her down already or put a bullet in her. We have too much shit going on to worry about her ass. Our problems with the cartel affect the entire MC, she's a speck where this is all concerned. Our women don't need to be worrying about a loose cannon while we're out of town taking care of club business."

Swallowing, my throat grows tight at the thought of burying her. I have to figure out another way to get her to see reason. "I'll take care of it."

He nods. "Bet. Now, anything I'm missing that needs to be talked about?"

Sinner signals.

"Sin?"

"2 Piece getting more weapons in from the Russians?"

"Good question. Touch base with him and see if we have time to restock. I haven't heard of the Russians paying a visit lately, so it's a decent chance they have something in the works. If not, ask if they have anything their charter is selling that we can get. And ammo as well; we can never have enough of it."

Sinner concurs, "I'll get it sorted and hit up Smokey if they have anything worth purchasing."

"Good. If the Russians are planning to drop in, I want a fifty-Cal and a rocket launcher, or something similar. We need to go in with plans to fuck some shit up."

Smokey coughs, exhaling a cloud of smoke. "You planning on driving down there, kid? Ain't no way you can strap those to your bikes and not get hauled off by the law. Oath Keepers don't have everyone in their pockets, ya know."

Viking huffs. "I'll make a prospect drive if needed. I'm not worrying about the little shit right now. We need to execute the bigger plan."

Odin speaks up, disagreeing. "You should be, brother. We have enough of a heads-up to cover our bases instead of going in half-cocked and shit. There's enough of us to take care of it all."

Viking glares. "You wanna sit in my motherfuckin' chair?"

Odin's hands shoot up, placating. "I'm just suggesting, Vike. Calm the fuck down."

"I agree with one aspect. There's enough of us sitting around this table to make sure all the small shit is squared away. We don't need a color-coded checklist with fucking designated chores. Put your colored pencils away and check for your balls, little brother."

The table cracks up, and Odin rolls his eyes. Poor kid will always be the younger brother around here with Viking in charge. VP or not, he's still the youngest sitting at the table.

Chaos asks, "You have a spot picked out for us?"

Viking shakes his head, taking a hefty gulp of his bottled water. "I know it's on the border. We'll hear more before we head out. Spider's checking in with me on it daily."

We sit back, getting quiet, lost in our thoughts of what's to come.

He finishes. "If there's nothing else, let's get the fuck out of here. We've all got plenty of shit to do, I'm sure. I sure as fuck do."

Various brothers nod.

"Before we clear out, I need to know if everyone's on board with this Mexico business." He peers around the table. "My vote is aye."

Odin: "Aye."

Me: "Aye."

Torch: "I should be going," he grunts. "I'm the death dealer, it's my job, but I respect your orders, so you'll get an aye from me."

Nightmare: "I've got your back. Always. I say we fuck them all up for good. My vote is fuck, yes."

Chaos: "Aye, brother."

Smokey coughs out an, "Aye. I'll look after your women." I roll my eyes. The dude is an ancient pervert. He's always been that way.

Saint: "Aye."

Sinner: "Aye."

Mercenary: "Aye."

Viking lifts the gavel. "It's done. Now get the fuck out." He slams it down, the noise echoing through the small room Viking's designated strictly for church.

We make our way into the bar. Usually, we drink and celebrate a bit after we have church, but in this case, most of the brothers take their leave to go find their respective women.

"You good?" I ask Torch, and he shrugs, plopping down on the leather couch. Honey rushes over with a couple of beers.

"Thanks, babe," I acknowledge, and she preens.

She goes to sit down, but Torch sends her a death glare, and she scatters.

"You're in a mood," I comment. He's never one for Honey's company, but he usually keeps his issues to himself so she can hang on another brother.

"I could do more if I was riding out with the club. I should have Viking's back on this, not leashed up like the club's fucking dog."

"I get it. I'm usually the one ordered to stay behind. I'd be too distracted if I was here with Amelia. Besides, you can protect the compound better than I was ever able to. I used to think my spot was useless, but it's not. You keep everything we care about safe. If it's Viking you're worrying about, well, he'll do whatever he wants, regardless if you're there or not."

"You want me to kill the principal and get her out of the way for you?" he probes, and my protective instinct flares. That's the last thing I want at the moment.

It must be all the time I've spent with Princess over the years that's made me feel this way inside over hurting women. I wouldn't have cared much in the past—out of sight, out of mind. That doesn't seem to be the case now, though. Anything happening to Amelia Stone has me wanting to hurt someone, and that detail freaks me the fuck out.

"I've got her. Speaking of, I need to talk to Princess. I'll catch you later."

He nods, letting me go without saying anything else.

I head for Viking's office. Princess is in there painting her toenails. The smell makes me cringe; that shit has to be toxic. I'll never understand how females can sit and inhale that crap and not catch a contact high.

"'Sup, P."

"Hey. You guys are done with church already?"

I nod.

"Everything okay?"

"I need you to do something for me."

Her brows raise, and she stares at me, waiting.

I admit, "The principal needs to shower...she hasn't since I brought her here."

"Uh, and why can't you help her?"

"I'm trying to give her space." I shrug.

"Is she still fighting with you? Wait a second...have you touched her?"

I shake my head.

"Not at all?" she questions, her eyes widening with shock.

I choke out a quick, gruff, "No."

"I can't believe you haven't slept with her already. You sleep with everyone! Well, anyone who isn't an ol' lady anyway. Has she friend-zoned you or something?"

With a groan, I swipe my hand over my face. I mutter a dejected, "Of course I'm not friend-zoned, damn it."

"She really has you shaken up, huh?" Her lips twist into a smirk. She's loving this shit.

"Amelia has this perception that men like me are her enemy. I already told you all of this shit the other day."

"And let me guess, you're trying to prove her wrong?"

I nod, sending her an incredulous look. "Yep, she is wrong."

"I know she is." Princess easily agrees, her smirk turning to a serious frown. "But you're being too soft on her." She pauses to blow on her nails for a beat then continues. "A woman like her, from what you've told me, needs to be pushed. You need to cross her boundaries, not tiptoe around them. She needs to be challenged, or she'll get bored...just like you."

"I'm liable to scar her for life or some shit."

She snorts, rolling her eyes. She's like a bratty younger sister sometimes. "What's so different about her, Blaze? You've never blinked in the past when it's come to women. You sleep with a different one every chance you get. Even *I* know that. Now this one, you have in your bed for multiple days, and you haven't so much as touched her?"

"I've never given a fuck before." The words rush from me, exasperated. "I go for a piece of ass because that's what I want."

"And you don't want that from her?"

"Of course, I do. I mean...fuck! That didn't come out right." I shake my head, tapping my fingers on my jean-clad thigh. *How can I say this without sounding like a dick?*

"She has you twisted," Princess quietly resolves.

P's completely right. I concede, releasing a sigh. "I need you to push her for me."

She grins, closing her polish bottle and stands. "I think I have something in mind."

I watch as she rounds Viking's enormous desk and digs through a drawer, careful not to jack up her nails. She finds what she's looking for, closes the drawer, and steps back around wearing a wide smile.

"What is it?" I ask, and she holds her hand in my sight. She palms a black and red ball gag. I should invest in one of these—can't say I'm surprised to see Vike has one in his office.

"I'm going to take her voice from her and make her feel. She'll shower, but I'm going to have some fun with her too."

"You better not piss your ol' man off. I'll be the one who pays for it, and cousin or not, he still hits fucking hard."

Her tinkle of a laugh rings through the office, glee filling her at my possible ass kicking. "I'll let him know what I have in mind, so he won't hurt you...not too bad, anyhow."

I rake my hand through my blond locks and mutter, "Great...just great."

"Hey, you want me to get her all shaken up, right? And I'm not a man, so she can't blame her emotions on that cop-out. Maybe we should've gone about this differently when you brought her in. Let me mess with her, and you'll look like the hero."

"Don't fuck her up, P. She already jacked her wrists to shit."

She giggles, delight shining in her gaze. "I won't, she'll be shaken up, but not from violence. Trust me."

"I do," I reply, and it's the truth. This chick is like my little sister. Now, what she'll do with Amelia is another thing altogether. Princess can be sweet or a hellion depending on her mood. I've witnessed firsthand her try and shoot her ol' man when he pissed her off enough. I wouldn't put it past her to hurt a bitch who's been screwing with members of the club. That's toying with her family, and she's protective of us all.

"I'll take care of her, don't you worry." She winks, and I cringe a little at her term.

"Don't shoot her," I grumble.

"I won't, I'm bringing the gag so she can't sass me. No need to worry about me hurting her."

I nod. She grins broadly and sways her hips as she leaves me in the office alone, wondering what in the hell her plan is. The bitch is crazy, so Amelia's in for it, that much I already know.

Amelia

I must've dozed off as I'm awoken by my head being moved. My lids part expecting Blaze, but I meet a stunning woman's gaze instead. She's leaning over me, pushing something between my lips. Before I can get my wits and protest, she's snapped it in place. Her icy pale platinum locks tickle my skin. Her hair must be long enough to touch her behind, and she's someone I'd expect to see on a runway, not in a biker club. Her ample chest brushes my forehead as she leans in closer to check over my wrists.

"Hmm, he didn't do too bad, I suppose," she comments, more to herself.

She leans away, lightly brushing her fingertips over my cheek. She's got some sort of gag in place, and I'm doing my best to not freak out and overreact just yet. I won't lie, the presence of another woman is comforting. I know that's ignorant of me to experience any sort of comfort in this place, but I can't help but feel a touch of hope she'll have pity on my situation.

"You're a beauty. No wonder why these men don't know how to deal with you," she murmurs.

I swallow, my throat growing dry. Maybe my hope was misplaced, and I should be wary of her instead. It's not as if I can ask her for help or anything. The gag she's put in place has made sure of it. Was this Blaze's idea, or is she acting all on her own?

"My brother doesn't want to touch you, but I think that's what you need the most." She winks, and I shake my head no. "You don't think so?" She raises a brow, and I shake my head again. A tinkling laugh escapes her, and she leans in, brushing her nose against mine.

"Mm-mm, too bad I don't have the patience Blaze does. I could have a lot of fun with you. It's been a while since I've had a woman."

I don't know what to think of that comment. I've never looked at other women sexually. I mean, sure, I've noticed when they were curvy or beautiful, but I haven't thought of them sexually in the past. Thinking of her, in that sense, has my thighs surprisingly pressing together.

She loosens my leg ties enough so I can spread them about a foot apart. Moving to the closest side of the bed, she grabs below my wrists. "I'm helping you up and taking you to the shower. You've been lying here in Blaze's bed, and you're starting to smell like him. It's time we get you cleaned up, so he notices you're a woman again."

I squint at her, not understanding her meaning or why she cares. She helps pull me up, wrapping her arms around my waist. She takes small steps so I can slowly shuffle toward the bathroom. I'd be outraged right now if it were a man holding my naked body like this, but the fact that she's a woman has me less tense.

"You need to be cleaned up and looking sexy for him, so he breaks his rule of not touching you."

I shake my head adamantly. I don't want that. Not at all. I wish I could talk, but I can't. I settle for making a displeased grumble sound around the ball in my mouth. She leans over a bit and turns the shower knob; it blasts the cold water into the tub, and I patiently watch as she keeps her hand under the water until she deems it a decent temperature. This is going to be awkward; I haven't had any help in this department since I was a child. Unless she unties me, all I can do once I'm in there is rinse off. I guess it's better than nothing, though. The woman grabs my wrists, careful not to touch the injured area and removes the bandages.

"We'll clean your wrists up after you shower and rewrap them, so they don't get infected."

I nod, wishing she'd take this thing off my face. She runs her hands through my hair, humming. I can't remember the last time someone touched me like that.

"I love this color. Is it yours?"

I nod again, not able to do much more. This is the strangest situation. I think she's trying to make me feel comfortable, but she keeps touching me, and it has me alert of every spot she grazes. My eyes grow wide as she begins to peel her clothes off as well. I make a whimpering sound, and she smiles softly.

"I'm not getting my clothes soaked. You won't be able to get in there by yourself, so we'll both be nakey." She giggles again and winks, clearly amused by my modesty. I've been stark naked for days now, but only in front of Blaze.

Tears build in my gaze. I'm not sure why. With Blaze, I fight against them, but around her, they crest so easily. I'm feeling too many things at once that it's overwhelming.

Her forehead scrunches. "Oh, honey. Shh, I won't hurt you as long as you behave yourself. Just relax. I'm here to help you be more comfortable. I know it's hard to believe anything in this situation, but you can trust me." Her voice grows serious as she declares, "However, I won't free you or anything like that, so don't get that false fantasy mixed with my kindness."

My tears fall at her admission. Of course, I'd had it buried in me somewhere that a woman would free me. I was wrong. Obviously, she's devoted to the bikers, or else I doubt Blaze would've allowed her in here with me. The knowledge is disheartening. It makes me feel like he was telling me the truth when he said no one outside this room would help me. *I don't know how I'm going to get myself out of this mess. Where do I even begin?*

I watch as she steps under the water. She's completely comfortable with her nudity, and I can understand why. She's gorgeous. The human body is an amazing thing, and hers was no doubt created as a temptation for everyone. I can't help but wonder if she's this way naturally or if she's undergone surgeries to look as she does. It's shallow to think that way, but I can't help but wonder. Her chest is overly full and perkier than mine. Her waist is tiny, and her hips are the perfect width that, when she walks, I'm sure she has everyone's attention.

I try not to stare too openly, though I find myself desiring to do so. I don't know what's gotten into me. I never act this way toward women. It must be the circumstances.

"Step up inside the tub, and I'll hold onto you, so you don't slip and fall," she instructs, reaching for me again.

I do as she says, shuffling the few paces closer to the shower and step inside, right in front of her. The water beats down on my bed sore body. *Jesus, I had no idea how much I needed this until now. It feels wonderful, even if I am kidnapped and tied up. Now, if I could brush my teeth as well, I'd be feeling even better.*

The water runs over my back, and I close my eyes, tipping my head back under the warm relief. My hair has been itchy all mussed up from the bed, and this is a sweet relief. The warm droplets feel divine peppering against my scalp.

"I'm going to wash you now."

That's something I wasn't expecting. I keep my eyes closed but nod, wanting this grimy feeling on my body to go away. I hear the snap of her opening and closing bottles. I wish I knew what to call her, rather than just the woman...even if it's only to myself in my head. I thought it was difficult being tied up, but taking my voice away as well has me scatterbrained. It's hard to think and concentrate on anything when all I want to do is speak.

"Keep your eyes closed," she orders and has me take a step forward, out of the spray. It still powers down on my behind, just not over my hair or shoulders.

I don't know how she could know that I need my head scratched. I can't gesture to anything, as I have my back to her. I do as she instructs and relish in her fingers, massaging my hair with the shampoo. The clean scent fills the shower, and I find myself feeling grateful for her touch, for her kindness. I groan around the gag. I can't thank her, but at least she'll know I'm enjoying the light scratch of her nails and soft massage of my scalp. I wonder if she's done this in the past with others. I can't think like that. I can't go there now, or I'll freak myself out all over again.

Her hands pull my shoulders until I step back under the full spray, and then she's running her fingertips through my hair, rinsing it clean. When she's satisfied with it, she pushes me forward again, tugging a comb through to release the knots. More snaps of a bottle opening and closing, then her small hands are rubbing soap over my shoulders. She massages as she goes, my head falling forward to hang with the amazing feelings she's eliciting throughout my tense, sore muscles.

I groan again, louder this time, and she chuckles behind me. "You must be aching," she mentions and rubs over my back, paying special attention to where my neck and shoulders meet.

I draw in a quick breath in the next second when her hands come around the front of my body, further alarming me. She hugs me from behind, her breasts pressing against my back. She builds up the suds against my belly before moving upwards to run her fingers over my chest. She palms my breasts, massaging, then rubbing her palms lightly across my nipples repeatedly. The sensations are intense, especially mixed in with the steam and heat from the water. *When was the last time I was touched like this? If ever? I can't remember, and I can't do a thing to stop it.* I bite down on the ball, understanding why it was put in place.

"You have perfect tits," she compliments breathily, her lips close to my earlobe. "I couldn't stop staring at them when I noticed you lying in Blaze's bed, napping. I knew I had to touch them."

My thighs squeeze against each other. I shouldn't be feeling so turned on by another woman, but I can't deny what she's doing to my body with her soft touch. My head falls back a bit once more, needing to draw in a deep breath. If my mouth were free of the gag, I'd most likely be panting at this point. My temperature's on fire.

Her hands shift lower, passing over my belly button again; they seem to keep growing sudsier. Then she's moving farther south and cupping between my thighs. I suck in a quick, shaky breath at her touch. My legs part, without much internal protest, surprisingly. Part of me wants to protest that this is all so wrong, but I've been kidnapped—regular words and thoughts don't count here. Nothing is in my control, and that's both terrifying and freeing.

I whimper behind the gag, then her lips are there, softly pressing to my neck. I don't know what to make of her tender kiss; it rattles me further.

"You need this, probably more than anyone realizes. I won't hurt you, don't think that." She reminds me as her palm begins to rub me, using the soap to glide back and forth over my clit. My head falls back to rest against her shoulder as I give in, realizing I have no choice in this. I'm going to enjoy her caress instead of allowing it to victimize me. I'm strong enough to not let her or anyone else shatter me into pieces here. "That's it, beautiful, let me make you feel good."

My thighs spread as much as my restraints will allow them to, offering her better access. She takes every bit and uses it to her advantage. Mere moments pass, and I'm a total shaking bag of nerves on the verge of an intense orgasm. My hips thrust, moving with her slippery hand, seeking more friction. I'm shameless in my pursuit of a release. She said she wouldn't hurt me, and I need this, whatever this is. Maybe it makes me stupid to be so open and vulnerable to her, but I can't bring myself to consider it or the repercussions right now.

"I wish I could slide my fingers and tongue inside this pretty peach, but my brother would kill me for breaching your hole," she whispers throatily, and it's my undoing. The picture she's painted in my mind has me spiraling, losing the last bit of control I'd possessed. Out of nowhere, an image of Blaze assaults me. I think of him catching her licking me...down there. It's so utterly forbidden, the thought's completely unlike me, but it's a turn on like no other as well.

Moaning around the gag, I ride out my orgasm as she dutifully rubs me until completion. She's holding me firmly to her, and I'm grateful for her embrace as my body is turning into Jell-O. She's massaged my head, tickled my scalp, rubbed the soreness from my neck and back, and given me the first orgasm I've had in a very long time. I'd guess it was too long, too, as it took her only seconds to have me shaking like it was my first time feeling the wave of bliss.

I'm panting, my cheeks flushed, with my body turning warm all over as she finishes her task of washing and rinsing me off. I turn my head enough to finally catch a good look at her. She reaches behind her, turning the shower off. I follow her every move with my droopy, sated gaze. I feel like I just ran a marathon, and I haven't done a thing since arriving except sleep and then stand here. She leans back up, reaching her full height. She takes me in and grins widely.

"You're even prettier like that. God, just wait until Blaze gives you an orgasm and sees you like this. The man will be even more smitten than he already is."

Her words aren't lost on me, and I scrunch my nose up. She must be wrong; she has to be. Blaze doesn't see me like that.

She giggles gleefully. "If he wasn't, you'd be locked in the basement, tied down to a hard chair, with the prospects feeding you bread and water all day."

My expression slackens, my face paling.

She shrugs and grabs a towel. "It's true. Instead, he has you sleeping in his bed and asking me what he should do with you. He told me he hasn't even touched you sexually yet. Blaze has gotten better where women are concerned, but he's not that saintly. He'd have at least groped you and threatened you multiple times by now if you were anyone else. For some reason, he's babying you. Which offers more evidence that he's got it for you, and if I had to guess, I'd say it's pretty bad."

My stare finds the carpet, my cheeks feeling a bit warm and tingly all over again. *Do I want him to like me like that?*

"Oh my God!" she declares loudly and gushes, "I was right! You totally like him back. Holy shit."

I go to shake my head to quickly disagree, but she raises an eyebrow, effectively stopping my dispute. This woman is good; she can see through everything. How can she possibly know so much and not be around us?

"It's okay, you know, thinking that a biker is sexy. I'm married to one—I know how they can drive you absolutely mad, but at the same time make you want to sit on their face and ride it. There's just something about an outlaw that has the overwhelming power to make a woman get wet. They're brash, hard men, but their overbearing nature is so fucking sexy when you get past them believing that they know everything."

"Hmph," I strive to argue, but nothing I say will make any possible sense with this stupid ball in my mouth.

She smirks. "That gag is teaching you how to keep your mouth positioned. You'll thank me when you finally give in and suck Blaze's cock, you know." She winks. "My ol' man had me wear it in the early stages of our relationship. His cock is huge, so I needed all the help I could get. Let's just say, he's one satisfied man."

I huff, shooting her a bored look. I shake my head with disagreement. *There's no way I'm ever putting my mouth anywhere near that man's member.* She just laughs and shakes her head back at me, like I have no idea what I'm talking about.

She hangs the towel up and runs her gaze over my dry nakedness. Her irises have heat reflecting in them, and there's not a doubt in my mind that she wants to do more than our short shower activity. I can't believe the thought of it doesn't bother me more. It should, but the truth is, I enjoyed it immensely. I'm succumbing to the circumstances already, and I mustn't allow myself to become a product of my environment like this striking woman seems to have.

"All right, principal Amelia, let's get you back on the bed and comfortable. You certainly smell good. I need to buy some of that soap for my shower."

I shake my head again, tears working their way to blur my vision once more. I don't want to go back to bed. I've been lying there for days. I think it's been two days, but with the drugs, I could be on day three or four and not even know it. When your mind is hazy and you lie in bed night and day, things begin to blend together and not in a good way. I can't believe I don't have a better grasp on things. I'm strong and capable but put me out of my element, and I'm like an elephant in the middle of the ocean, trying not to sink before hitting land.

She tilts her head, growing concerned, or at least pretending to be. "Oh, sweetie, it's not that bad, I promise. How about we sit you on the big chair while I get your wrists all wrapped up with fresh bandages, and if you want to stay there when I finish, you can do that. If you're too uncomfortable sitting there, then I'll help you lie back down. If we're lucky, you'll come to your senses sooner than later and give in to Blaze. Maybe if you give up some pussy, he'll decide to keep you around, and you can join the other whores. I've heard them say he's a good lover. One of the girls is practically in love with him. The man's oblivious, though. He'd never notice her like that, so you're a good contender for him."

I gasp, my eyes wide at her flippant comment about me becoming a whore. I was right; they *are heathens* if they have those type of women just hanging out around here. I hope there aren't drugs and needles or whatever lying around anywhere. However, I should come to expect that, I suppose. This situation just went from bad to worse. Is this my reality now? Die or turn into a whore for men to use as they wish? What did I ever do in my past life to deserve this?

The blonde pulls her clothes on and helps me shuffle to Blaze's chair. I scan everywhere as much as I can, for signs of discarded paraphernalia. Blaze seems far too alert to be on anything, though he admitted to drugging me, so I wouldn't be surprised to find something in here. The thought of contracting diseases or whatever else has me on edge even more now. Like possible rape or death wasn't enough.

"I can see your mind working a hundred miles a minute. Try to calm down, or you'll give yourself a panic attack. Like I said, he doesn't pay the whore much consideration; he's far more interested in you. Well, he won't actually admit it, but I can tell. I know him better than most around here."

Her flippant comment grabs my attention. I can't help but wonder how she knows him so well. She called him her brother. Maybe they really are siblings, and it's not just an endearment? That could explain why she's the one in here helping me shower and such, but who knows. I'm not sure of what to think here, with any of them. Blaze has called several people his brothers, so I'm confused when it comes to people related to him by blood.

Above all else, I can't seem to stop wondering if they're ever going to let me out of this room. I want my clothes back; I can't allow others to see me like this. If Blaze takes me out of here, will he force me to stay naked? I'd be grateful to have some underwear and a shirt at this point. I thought I was comfortable with my nudity in the past, but clearly, I had no idea just how wrong I was believing that nonsense.

My gaze remains trained on her movements, watching as she applies ointment to my scratched-up wrists and carefully rewraps them. She's much tidier than Blaze was and manages to tear the tape rather than use her teeth. I wonder if she's locked up inside this place all the time as well. Do they keep all of their women on some sort of lock-down? It wouldn't surprise me; they remind me of cavemen. Besides, I think I'd have seen her around town at some point if it weren't the case. Though with them located out of town a bit, there's a good chance I haven't noticed many of the people that come here.

She stands, satisfied with her work. "There, you're all set. Do you want to stay sitting over here?"

I nod. I'd prefer to sit up for a while. My back and neck ache from constantly lying down. Besides, what if I get stuck on my back and I choke on my own spit or something? With how my luck seems to be going recently, I wouldn't put it past happening.

"Okay, then. I'll let Blaze know, so he doesn't ask you twenty questions on how you ended up over here."

She's going to leave me here, alone, again. Her presence offers me a sense of comfort for some reason. I don't want her to leave me. I shake my head, eyes pleading for her to stay, for her to free me.

Please, please, please stay here.

"I have other things I need to take care of, but I'll check on you again. I promise, okay?"

My disappointed gaze falls to the floor, but I nod anyway. I'm upset, but hopefully, she stays true to her word and returns. I don't want to push her too much and have her not return at all. I lift my eyes, watching as she walks away. She turns one last time, glancing back at me and blowing a kiss before closing the door behind her.

The lock clicks into place, and my head falls back against the cushioned chair. I sigh around the uncomfortable ball in my mouth and close my eyes. I'm not a praying person, nor much of a believing one. In this case, though, I'll try anything to help me out of this situation. With that thought, I begin to pray for some sort of help. There's nothing else I can do; Blaze has all of the control.

Blaze

"She's all fresh and clean," Princess announces once she finds me in the bar busy drinking a beer.

"You put her in the shower?"

She tips her pale blonde head in a nod. "I also loosened her legs up a bit so she could kind of walk; otherwise, I couldn't have gotten her into the bathroom by myself. I didn't think you'd want me to voluntold a prospect to do the job."

"I had them tied up in case she started kicking, and you were right about that. The prospects need to stay the fuck away from Amelia."

"Yeah, I figured. I have an idea if you'll hear me out?"

"Of course," I easily concede.

"I saw this on a movie once..." I send her a look about to cut her off, and she talks faster. "But what if you tie a rope across the room and hook her hands over it? If there's some slack in it, then she could walk to the bathroom, sit down or lie down while you're not in the room. You could untie her legs, and even if she tries anything, she won't get far with her hands tied over a lead."

I can't believe I'm even considering something she said she saw it in a movie. It kind of makes sense, though. "How would I secure it?" I ask aloud, already beginning to picture it in my mind.

She shrugs and plops down on the couch beside me. "Maybe under the bathroom sink or behind the toilet. Do you have something in your room you could secure it to? It's not like she's very strong...well, not strong enough to pull it out of the wall."

"Hmm. I could find one of the wall studs and install a couple of metal bars. It'd only cost about ten or twenty bucks, and then I'd have something to attach the ropes to and give her the length I'd want her to have."

"You should do it," she urges, and I crack a grin.

"I kidnapped her, and now you want me to give her freedom?"

"No. I know better than to meddle in club business. I'm just saying that a little slack would go a long way with her. She seems to have one of those minds where she automatically works out the worse scenario and panics. I know you said she's stubborn and strong-willed, but you've made her vulnerable. If you offer her a little something, it'll make it so you don't come off quite so evil in her eyes."

"Hmph," I grumble. I know how this principal is already; she's been loud and clear about how she feels. "I doubt that P. The woman thinks all alpha men are the enemy, and that includes me as well."

"Like I was just saying, she automatically reverts to the worst case. She likes to be in control, but you need to show her that you're in charge of everything, including her well-being and that she can trust in you to take care of everything. It won't be easy, but you can do it. Don't be too headstrong with her, or she'll shut you out. Give her the rope lead and some attention. You're one of the most charismatic guys I know. Show her that side, too, and she won't be able to deny you."

"She can't deny me when she's tied up anyway," I mutter gruffly and take another swig from my beer.

"Obviously, you don't want things to be like that. Otherwise, you'd never have involved me in the first place. You asked for my help, and I'm giving it to you." She crosses her arms over her chest.

I exhale, running my fingers through my lightly gelled golden locks. "Fine...all right, P. I'll give your suggestions a go, but if she doesn't show me anything in return, then I'm going to have to work somethin' else out."

"What are you going to do?" She wrinkles her forehead, staring me down.

With a shrug, I admit, "I don't know. In the past, I'd hurt women that didn't comply with my orders, but I don't want to be that man anymore."

"You aren't, Blaze." Her hand falls to my arm, concern filling her gaze. "Jekyll made you think those things were okay, but you've changed. I haven't heard or witnessed you hurt a female since you came to the Oath Keepers years ago. I was the last, remember?"

I swallow, my throat feeling tight at the memory. "I could never forget or forgive myself," I confess, and her hand squeezes me.

"Stop thinking about it. You're my brother. I've forgiven you and moved on, and you need to do the same. You're not that person anymore."

I nod, even though I don't know if I'll ever be able to actually do it—forgive myself and move past it. I deserve to be punished.

Princess leans in, hugging me. "I love you, Blaze. She'll come to her senses and realize you're not what she thinks you are."

With a nod, I gruffly reply, "Thanks, P." That's about as affectionate as I'll get with her. Viking would castrate me otherwise. She's his property, and I fully respect that. I do love her as my younger sister, just as all the brothers around the MC should. She's earned our respect and admiration as the queen bee around here. Anyone ever hurts her, and it'll be a full-fledged act of war against the club.

With only a few days before we're supposed to ride out and get into some shit, I head to the hardware store to pick up everything I need. I can't believe I'm going out of my way for this ungrateful woman. I hope Princess is right, and I'm not putting in the effort for nothing. The store clerk gives me a wary look when I check out, probably thinking I'm up to no good. If he knew the truth of the matter, he'd probably piss his pants. I've been a kidnapper for over half my life, so it doesn't faze me. Civilians, on the other hand, are a different story.

I pack away everything in my saddlebags and make my way back to the compound. I pass a few sheriff's deputies on my ride home and send up a salute in acknowledgment. We're on good terms with them, but I can't help but be entertained at the thought I have a woman tied up in my room, and they haven't the faintest clue about it. We've paid them handsomely to look the other way as far as we're concerned. The club also helps keep the peace in central Texas with gangs and hard drugs. It allows them a cushy job with incentives while on duty. Lucky bastards.

"Blaze." A prospect greets me as I pull up to the perimeter gate. It's one of the twins, and I haven't the faintest fucking idea which one he could be. I don't give a fuck what Torch says, these kids sound and look the same to me. They need name patches; otherwise, I'll just stick to calling both of them prospect, shithead, or any other name that comes to mind.

"'Sup," I chin-lift, not in the mood to chitchat.

There's a girl giggling and feeling up the twin's brother. The dude is completely distracted from what he's supposed to be doing.

"The fuck's goin' on around here?" I bark loudly over the rumble of my engine. My brow lifts with irritation.

He shrugs, obviously not understanding that they're fucking up right about now. "She wanted in, so we're testing her out. Making sure she's really a club whore looking for work before radioing and bothering anyone inside."

I huff, my nostrils flaring. "That's not your place, fuck stick. You two shitheads are supposed to be paying attention to your surroundings. That doesn't mean you wait here and open the fucking gate to whoever moseys along; it means you keep alert and watch for anything that could be creeping up. This bitch isn't your concern. Besides, what if she was a decoy? Use your brain, numbnuts. You text or radio into the brother on gate security, and he'll come check her the fuck out. You get me? Should I hit up the prez and let him know you're far too interested in some snatch to do your motherfucking job?"

"Fuck," he huffs, throwing a glare back at his brother. "I'll text them right now."

I nod. "You gonna clue your brother in, or should I?" I ask with a threatening tone. He doesn't want me to have to point it out again. My cousin will listen if I think these two should take a fucking hike. You want to be a member of this club, you have to pay your dues, put in your time, and make us confident we can trust you. Otherwise, you're no good to us. This is club life, but it's also our family.

"I'll take care of it, Blaze. You won't have to mention it again."

"Yeah?" I rev my engine.

He nods, his Adam's apple bobbing as he swallows. "Won't happen again; you have my word."

"That's what I wanna hear. Now open the fucking gate and do your job."

He swiftly steps over to the new lock we had installed last weekend. It scans his eye, and he types in his temporary code. It clicks open, then the two gates make a whirring sound as they open, and I slowly cruise through.

The new lock we installed has a scan log that notes whoever comes as well as a heat sensor. If a body's dead and cold, it won't open, so rival clubs can't kill one of us and use our eye to open the lock. It was insanely expensive, but when you have a compound full of the most important people in your life and have been hit hard in the past, it's well worth it. Ever since Nightmare's kid was kidnapped and we were fucked up, we're always looking for ways to improve our security. I'm not afraid to admit that it has me sleeping easier at night. I had some dark fucking dreams for a minute after I nearly died. No one around here knows that bit of truth, however. Those thoughts and memories are mine alone.

Toeing my kickstand down, I kill the engine and hop off. Grabbing my purchases from the hardware store, I hurry through the clubhouse to my room, not stopping to chitchat with any of the brothers. Most of them are busy anyhow with getting shit together for this run that's coming up quick. As long as I'm strapped with plenty of ammo, then I'm not worried about anything other than my captive principal. Knowing she's in there waiting for me has my stomach jumbled up. It's like having a shiny new toy I get to play with all by myself.

I practically burst through my door, bags in hand. Amelia's head snaps up at the commotion. She meets my gaze, and I barely manage to hold back a pleased groan. Not only did Princess clean her up and keep her naked, but she also has her gagged. I wasn't lying about her being a shiny new toy. She's like a present just waiting to be thoroughly fucked. The hardest part of all is not touching her like I want to. The bad man deep down in me whispers to hold her down and fuck her senseless, but that's not who I am anymore.

"You all right?" I gruffly ask, gritting my teeth as my cock grows into a semi.

Tears well in her eyes, her forehead scrunching. I'm confident she's got something to say. That's one trait she's had consistently since we first met. The bitch is mouthy.

"Hold on, sweetheart; I'll help you out." Closing the door behind me, I set the bags down right inside and head for the naked beauty.

Stopping in front of her, I murmur, "Hold still. I don't want to yank your hair or pinch you."

She blinks, holding my gaze a moment before I realize she's keeping still. Chuckling to myself, I reach around and carefully unsnap the gag. Holding it in one hand, I use my free hand to lightly rub her jaw and temples. I'm sure she's sore from having the gag in place for most of the day.

Her eyes close and she leans her head back. I take a moment to let her get her bearings and fetch her a small cup of water from the bathroom sink.

"Take a few sips of this and lick your lips. You'll feel better."

She does as I say and whispers a soft, "Thank you."

"I didn't know P had left you like this, or I'd have come sooner to check on ya."

She takes a few more drinks of the water, and I balance the cup between her hands so she can sip as she pleases. "Where were you?" she eventually asks.

I tilt my head at her nerve to ask me anything. She's not in the position to question me, nor is she my ol' lady. My prez and ol' lady would be the only two people I'd worry about giving my location, not a naked, kidnapped woman tied up in my room.

She nods to the bags. "You went shopping?"

"Oh, yeah. The hardware store."

She bites her bottom lip, and I know she's making herself refrain from interrogating me any further. She's used to being the one in charge and having everyone bow to her inquisition. I'm not them; here, I'm in control. She watches with rapt attention as I dump out the bags and go to my closet. I dig out my drill and bits. Amelia notices the thick rope and stutters, "Uh...m-more ropes?"

She probably thinks this is going to turn into some **BDSM** freak show, but she couldn't be more wrong. Sure, I like a little spice in my sex life just like every other man out there, but not that sort of thing. I nod, admitting, "I'm not tying them around you, so relax. You want me to help you lie down, or are you okay sitting in the chair still?"

"I'd like to lie down."

Rather than say anything, I set the drill down and come back over to her. I don't give Amelia a chance to walk or make much of a decision as I tug her up into my arms. I do it too quickly for her to protest, not that she has much sway in her opinions around me. Any excuse I can find to touch her or have her against me, I'm taking. She'll learn to get comfortable with my touch; even if I need to break her walls down slowly, I will. I was going to let her go after the two weeks, but at this rate, I may never release her. I want to keep her more with every hour that passes.

"Oomph," she mumbles as her body comes in contact with my much bulkier form. She's lucky I don't body slam her ass on that bed and take what I want. But no, I'm stuck on being the nice guy.

"Shh," I lay her down, princess style, noticing just how good she smells with my soap on her. She's sexy as fuck.

She hands me her empty cup, and I set it on my dresser. My eyes stay trained on her as I head back to the door and everything I'd dumped there.

The way she's laying, one of her legs has partially fallen open, giving me a peek at her pussy. I swallow as my throat dries, and my cheeks warm. I want to dip between those thighs and lick that little cunt until her pussy lips are pink and swollen, and she's exhausted from coming on my mouth multiple times.

"Blaze?" she calls, and my eyes find hers again. Hers are dilated, telling on herself that she damn well knows exactly what I was looking at.

I clear my throat and manage to work out a gruff, "Yeah?"

"Thank you," she says, and it isn't lost on me how she presses her thighs together. Could she be thinking about me all up in that pussy too? If she's not letting me pound her soon, I'm going to work Honey to death on sucking my cock dry. I gotta have some sort of relief to clear my head and remain patient with the principal. I can't afford to lose myself with her, it'll ruin every bit of traction that I've gained with her.

I get to work, busily installing the first bar for this contraption Princess told me about. Once it's in place, I secure the rope around it and step toward the bed.

Amelia shoots me a panicked gaze. "Blaze?"

"I'm not wrapping it around you," I explain, questioning myself on why I give a fuck if she's upset about something. "It's to feed through your arms. I'll free your legs afterward, and you'll be able to move around the room and to the bathroom easier."

She remains quiet and watchful as I put the thicker rope between her tied wrists. I find a stud in the bathroom and install the other bar, looping the rope around it as well. Once everything's secure, I move back to the bed and untie her legs. She immediately moves to flex them outward but stops and slams them closed once realization dawns that she was spreading her legs open for me.

"T-this doesn't mean..." she begins, taking in my heavy breathing,

"What?" I sit on the bed next to her knees.

"You wanted my legs free?" she asks, worry filling her expression as she glances from me to her perfect creamy thighs.

"I told you, babe, it's so you're able to move around. You can get a drink from the sink or use the bathroom. Hell, you can burn a hole in the carpet pacing if you want. I don't give a fuck; it's meant to make things a little easier and comfortable on you."

She releases an exhale and finally concedes, "Thanks."

I nod. What the fuck am I supposed to say back about it? I've taken her and tied her up, and she's thanking me for letting her drink and go to the bathroom. It makes me feel kinda like a grade-A dick for not doing it sooner. Maybe Princess was right after all.

Standing, I peel my shirt off and toss it in the hamper located in my closet and then put my tools in the back of the top shelf. I don't want them anywhere she can reach them, even if it is just a drill and bits. In the past, I've witnessed my homie Twist use a drill to fuck some people up before. I'll never look at another tool the same way again.

Flicking my belt free, I tug my pants down and toss them in the closet with my shirt. Once I'm completely naked, I head for the shower, not hiding myself one bit. I want her to stare. I want her to think about my body. *I want to be on her mind, period.*

Sapphire Knight

Amelia

I'm lost in my thoughts, staring toward the bathroom when a billow of steam surrounds Blaze as he steps out of the shower. He quickly runs a towel over his exquisitely carved muscles, looking more and more like someone I'd see on a men's fitness magazine in the supermarket. He's just the bad boy version, something I foolishly believed I'd never be attracted to. Oh, how I was completely wrong on that account. It's okay if I look, right? It's not as if I've developed Stockholm Syndrome. I'm just admiring his body. It has to be from abstinence and nothing more. He's a criminal and zilch about that fact draws me to him, but his body...even his smile and the timbre of his voice. They do things to me that I shouldn't be thinking about in my situation, or ever for that matter.

"I have to sleep with this rope through my arms?" I eventually manage to ask, once I've recited the periodic table to get myself in check. Him untying my legs was an amazing feeling, but now that I've been lying here with this thick rope between my arms, it's beginning to agitate me as well. I realize I don't have much room to complain, but if I bring it to his attention, maybe he'll do something about it like he did with my legs.

He tosses the towel over the top of the shower and brushes his teeth without replying. Once that task is complete, which looked far too sexy to be so mundane, he swaggers toward me. I swallow a few times quickly, aware that I shouldn't be staring at him, yet not being able to make myself turn away. There's an enigma about him. Sure, it's infuriating, but it's also unbelievably attractive. I shouldn't think of him like that, period. He's a heathen lawbreaker, a biker...my kidnapper. I despise anyone like that. And he's so male, it makes me sick. But oh my, he is so ridiculously good-looking and mix in his deep voice...well, it gives me goosebumps—the good kind.

With that realization, I glance away, pinning my glare on the irritating rope. I won't give him the courtesy of looking him in the eye. "You're not afraid I'll attempt to wrap it around your head as you sleep?" I don't think there's enough slack, but maybe it'll motivate him to unhook me from it.

He snorts, completely sure of himself. I haven't met a more overconfident man in my life. It infuriates me that the thought of me harming him is completely outlandish to him. I'm not a violent person, but this is my life we're talking about here. He's taken me, stolen away my clothing and tied me up. I'm pretty sure that's grounds for me to fight back, however necessary.

"It's amusing how you still believe you have any chance when it comes to me. I told you, a woman like you, with no discipline and training, isn't a match for a man of my size. And, by the way, wrapping it around my head would do you no good. I'd maybe get some rope burn, which would only piss me off. You'd have to figure out how to get it around my neck and then be able to overpower me to strangle me from behind. Unless you train MMA, well, the chances aren't in your favor." He winks.

I bristle inside, fuming at his condescending tone. "Don't you dare belittle me," I spit.

He rolls his eyes, planting his gorgeous behind on the bed. "I'm tellin' you the truth. I say it because I've been fighting to survive for as long as I can remember. The instinct to kill is ingrained in my blood." He flicks his tormented azure gaze over me before muttering, "You're headstrong and opinionated, but you're no killer. Hell, you're too scared to have a child, you definitely wouldn't have the protective instinct to fight me and come out on top."

"I-I'm not scared to have a child." I sputter, arguing. "Why would I want to bring a human being into a male-dominated world? What if I have a daughter, she'd be subjected to everything in the world today. Or a son? I'd have to constantly be shielding him from temptation and then have men like you torment him for being what you've deemed a beta."

He huffs, shaking his head and lies back beside me. "That's where you're fucking twisted. You need men like me to teach your son how to live. You need men like me to protect your daughter from men worse than me. You're not in your fabricated little world anymore. You're in the real one now. Time to open your eyes and come to terms with reality. That shit you see on the news and preach at your anti-male meetings ain't real. It's a bunch of bullshit made up to create division amongst people. We'd all survived together just fine for many years."

"Because men were always in charge."

"And many of those men helped fight to give you equal rights. Just because I'm a real fucking man doesn't mean I don't believe in equality for women."

My mind races at his last words. He really feels that way? But he's so overbearing and what about all the pregnancy stuff? "But you've said in the past you don't believe in artificial insemination and everything else against what I believe in. How can you change it now?"

"Oh, no," he grumbles. "I didn't change shit. You didn't want to listen to what I think or believe when I first met you. You took one look at me and made up your mind about me. I didn't say I don't believe in artificial insemination or anything else. I said a woman should have children the natural way, with a man. If you can't, then I one hundred percent support doctors stepping in to help it happen. I don't support women not including men altogether in the process though, we were created to procreate together. I never said feminists are wrong or bad, I said the ones who were anti-men were off their rocker. We don't *not* support women or want to keep them pregnant, barefoot, and in the kitchen. Believe it or not, many of us don't want to stand in front of you, but beside you. I'd only be in front of you if I needed to protect you."

I bite my bottom lip, unsure exactly how to reply. I want to argue with him, but what he said wasn't exactly a bad thing. "I'm tired of men like you trying to control everything."

He sighs. "Not all of us want to control everything. The majority of us want to be able to provide for our families and do what we want. You extremists are trying to take away our guns, our rights, and the American dream. We were fine before the news and social media stirred up this shit storm."

"Yeah, that's because of crazy people doing mass shootings."

"I'm beginning to think you're a fucking lost cause. Did you not hear anything I said to you?"

Does this mean he's going to kill me? Because I don't agree with him? I was just trying to talk, but I should've kept my thoughts to myself in fear for my life. "I heard you."

"Obviously you missed the part where I said we want to protect you. Not every person with a gun wants to hurt you. This is a prime example of why women need men. No matter how independent you all may be, we can make you feel safe. I'm not saying that to control you or get you all ruffled. It's the truth. We want to protect you and care for you. If your stubborn asses would get the crazy thoughts out of your head, we'd be able to do that. We'd be there in the middle of the night during a robbery to help you escape and take a bullet to keep you alive. Wouldn't you want to sleep easy at night, knowing someone has your back like that?"

I nod. Of course, what he said sounds nice, though I'm not sure how much truth is in his words. But it would be a relief, knowing someone wanted to keep me safe so fiercely. "I should take a self-defense class," I admit, thinking into it further.

I expect him to disagree, but he surprises me.

"You should. You should also get your permit and take shooting lessons at the range. Those beta males you surround yourself with damn sure won't be able to save you. They'll put on a pink pussy hat and hide behind you."

"I could protect them," I say, daring to offer a small smile.

He shakes his head. "Not like this, you couldn't. If you learned how to fight and concealed carry, then maybe. Until then, you'd both be easy pickings."

"Why do men have to think like that?"

"It's not just men, sweetheart; it's the world. I keep telling you to open your eyes. The news only gives you a smidge of the facts. Painting us out to be the bad guys isn't the answer. It's part of the problem."

I turn away from him, not wanting to discuss it anymore. He's put a lot of thoughts in my head that weren't there before, and I need time to process.

"Night, Amelia," he murmurs.

"Night, Blaze," I reply and close my eyes. For once, I'm not lying here terrified that I'll be killed or raped. As I fall asleep, I can't help but think that I don't have to worry about anyone trying to break into this crazy place. If it's full of men like Blaze, then they're trained and ready to protect who needs it and defend their home. I hadn't thought of this place as someone's home before, but now, I can see that's exactly what it is.

With a sleepy sigh, I relax as he pulls the fluffy comforter around us, and the soft hum of the air conditioner kicks on. The room grows chilly, but I'm warm from the blanket and Blaze's body heat. Wrapped up in his manly scent, I drift off to sleep.

Waking up, I notice multiple things at once. The warm breaths from Blaze's mouth that keep fluttering over the back of my neck. His face is on my pillow, tucked in close. His lips graze my skin occasionally, and the motion elicits goosebumps to cover me. His big, heavy arm is tucked around my middle, spooning me from behind. The heat coming off him is intense, but it's also kept me toasty all night.

The main thing that has me breathing shallowly is the blunt tip of his length. It's pressing into the apex of my thighs from behind. It's so close to my entrance, I could wiggle down a touch and slide right onto him. I wonder how he'd react if I did just that? The thought of it has wetness pooling below and my thighs clamping tighter, seeking some sort of relief. The movement has my muscles squeezing his tip, and my mouth parts to softly pant at the sensation.

Blaze groans behind me, and I stiffen up. Waiting a few beats, he doesn't say anything, he just goes back to breathing evenly. I flex my legs again, now curious if he'll make another noise from me squeezing him.

He responds with a soft moan, his lips caressing the back of my neck. In response, his hips thrust, pushing his head against my opening and my pussy contracts. Sex would be extreme with him; I know it. His length isn't super long, but he's girthy, and it'd leave a lasting impression behind. This is bad—so bad. I can't believe I'm even contemplating sex with him. After yesterday with that woman, things are different. At least with my body, it's like she's woken something up that was dormant. How can I even find this guy attractive in the least?

He is, though...he's ridiculously sexy. His hand flattens and runs over my abdomen. His fingertips stop below, his middle finger directly over my clit. He's not actually touching me down there, just hovering above. It's frustrating, I want him to put a bit of pressure. My thighs squeeze again, tugging at his length.

"Mm," he grumbles in his sleep and thrusts upward again. The motion has my pelvis tilting forward, and his finger grazes my clit.

My eyes clamp tight, my teeth nearly gritting with the divine sensation. That's it, though. He takes it no further, and I'm left exhaling in frustration. Have I really stooped this low? I'm essentially getting him to hump me so I can feel his fingers on me. Why is this happening to me? I'm supposed to hate him, not crave his touch! This wouldn't be so bad if I could reach down and take care of myself, but in this position, his stupid rope doesn't give me enough slack. It's all driving me a bit crazy.

With the next squeeze and Blaze's returning thrust, I shift my front toward the bed. His hand moves with my turn, and I shamelessly grind my clit against his fingers. Good thing he sleeps deeply or this could turn embarrassing very quickly. His breathing speeds up a little, but it's still the deep, sleepy inhales and exhales. His body remains still, so I move my hips some more, testing the limits. I feel like some sex-starved woman next to a very naked, ridiculously good-looking, virile male.

My mind runs wild, and I imagine him waking up and pinning me down, then thrusting into me from behind. It'd be a tight fit, but it'd be everything I needed at this moment. With the delicious image in place, I continue to swivel my hips. His fingers in the perfect position to rub my clit, back and forth. I clamp my teeth together to keep me from moaning. The sensations are even more intense than yesterday in the shower. *I have a ruthless biker's hand on my pussy, touching me, making me wet.* I release a whimper as my orgasm takes over, making everything else around me disappear. I ride his hand, working through my orgasm until I'm panting, and reality comes crashing back in.

I can't believe I just did that. Holding my breath, my body stills as I try to hear the man behind me. Is he awake? Did I jostle him too much and make a fool of myself at his mercy? He doesn't say anything, but I can no longer hear his steady breaths. They're ragged, and his cock stands to attention, even stiffer than before. I don't know how that's even possible, but the thing is like steel poking at the skin under my entrance.

He exhales heavily and scoops me to him tighter. His lips press more firmly against my neck. If I didn't know any better, I'd swear it was a kiss. That can't be right, though; he wouldn't be sweet on me like that. He doesn't strike me as a guy who'd be all lovey-dovey, but quick and hard. He's a man's man, and I can't forget that.

I must've dozed off because the next time I wake up, it's to the sound of the shower going, and the heater beside me is no longer there. The room is filled with the scent of his body wash. I inhale deeply, loving how it leaves me fuzzy-headed. It's like an aphrodisiac; whoever manufactured the scent knew what they were doing.

The comforter's gone, and my body's chilled, probably why I woke up in the first place. Blaze is infuriating, always leaving me in the nude. In the beginning, I thought it was so he could stare at me and rape me, but now I'm thinking it's for another reason entirely. If it weren't for me catching him staring between my legs last night and his hardness this morning, I'd be tempted to believe that he's not attracted to me at all. I don't know why the thought bothers me as much as it does. Besides, I'd be an idiot to not think he has a harem of women at his disposal. The realization should be reassuring, but it's not. It has the opposite effect on me, and that irks me like no other.

Moments later, he comes out of the shower, towel quickly swiping over his godly form. "You sleep better with your legs untied?"

he inquires. The man looks more attractive than last night, though the thought is ridiculous. He hasn't changed, but something in my mind seems to have flipped, and all I can think of is licking those droplets off his chiseled abs.

"Hm?" My eyelashes flutter as I cast my gaze over his impeccable physique. I take him in, inch by striking inch.

He clears his throat, and my eyes meet his. His eyebrow raises. "You sleep better?"

"Oh, umm," I move my legs together, then nod. "Yes, actually, I did. I'm not as stiff."

He nods in return. "Hungry?"

"Are you cooking?" I tease with the start of a smile.

He snorts. "Nah, but the club whores do."

It's like a bucket of cold water. Club whores. Did the woman insinuate yesterday that Blaze may keep me around to be one of them? There's no way I'll allow that to happen. I won't offer my body up and do whatever else they want me to. "No, most certainly not," I huff and cast my gaze off to the side.

I can still see him in my peripheral. His shoulders bounce, and he yanks on his clothes. They seem to be a nuisance to him; I wish I had that problem. "Suit yourself," he says, reaching down and tugging on his big black riding boots.

"A-are you leaving?" I ask, not ready for him to leave me alone already. I'm always stuck in this room by myself with nothing to distract me but my thoughts.

"I've got shit to do. You've got your lead now, so you can go to the bathroom, shower, or whatever. Use my toothbrush if you want."

I scoff in return, but he just shrugs, completely unperturbed with my rebuff.

"I'll have someone check on you later."

"A club whore?"

His stare finds mine, and he seems curious and confused all mixed together. "You're starting to sound like a jealous wife," Blaze states, and my mouth drops open. "I took you. You're mine now, remember that. You don't ask the questions, I do."

I glare in return, keeping my mouth screwed shut. He's such a chauvinist pig.

"I'll be back," are his parting words, then the door slams shut, leaving me in silence.

I'm able to make out the sound of his key entering the two-way deadbolt, and then I'm locked in—alone again.

Sapphire Knight

Blaze

I sit down hard on the barstool and gruffly order, "Frost, give me a fuckin' whiskey." I need something harder than my usual beer. Hell, at this rate, I need an entire bottle. That woman in my room has me all types of twisted up.

He nods, his eyes wide at my need for liquor this early in the day. I tend to stick to beer unless it's going to be a night full of partying, then I drink, smoke, snort, or whatever else seems good at the moment to get down with. Mornings are usually for coffee and Baileys or Bloody Marys. Not today, though.

The prospect sets down the rocks glass filled with two fingers worth of amber liquor. I instantly down it, gesturing for a refill. "I may need the bottle at this rate," I admit aloud.

A low whistle comes from my left, and then Odin's sliding into the seat beside me. "A little early, huh? Even for you." He smirks.

"Long night," I grumble. "Actually, a long night and a longer morning."

"Yeah? Not a good one, then?"

"Fuck you."

He chuckles. "The fuck's got your panties in a wad?"

"That bitch from the school."

"The principal?" His brow wrinkles.

I nod and chin-lift in the direction of our rooms. "You guys haven't seen her naked. Sexiest bitch I've ever fucking seen. And her mouth...God help me, she's gonna put me in an early grave."

"Doesn't sound so bad, brother."

"The hell it's not, I have to lay next to her ass all night long."

He shrugs. "She hot, but her pussy loose? You could lay elsewhere."

I shoot him a glare. For some reason, the thought of anyone talking about Amelia's pussy, even my blood cousin—my MC brother—it pisses me the hell off. "I wouldn't know, and I'm sleeping in *my* bed."

"What?" he exclaims, mouth hanging in surprise. "You've had her for, what...days now, right? You haven't tapped that ass yet?"

I shake my head, hanging it. "She doesn't want me...well, I thought as much until this morning. I don't know if that was me or something else, though."

"What happened this morning?"

I swear, if this fucker laughs, I'm going to punch him. "She kept wiggling around and shit made my cock hard as fuck. She didn't shy away from it, though. She kept moving her thighs together, squeezing my tip."

"Damn, brother," he grunts.

I nod. "I promised not to touch her from the start, so she'd quit freaking the fuck out. Anyhow, she ended up turning over. I had my hand over her before her squeezing had woken me up...the bitch was grinding against my hand, practically riding it. I wanted to put my fingers in her so bad and thrust into her ass while she was rubbing her pussy all over my hand."

"Holy fuck, Blaze. The fuck'd you do? You still didn't nail her?"

I shake my head, my body warm from the whiskey or her, who the hell knows. "I let her do her thing, she came all over my hand."

"Goddamn, brother. You're a better man than me; I'd have fed her my pipe."

"As soon as I knew she was asleep, I licked my fingers and jerked my dick. Mind you, I just jerked my cock the night before from seeing her fine ass tied up in my room."

"You need to get your dick wet, brother; you'll be all sorts of fucked up otherwise. You shouldn't be letting this bitch get the better of you."

"Trust me, man, it was the last motherfucking thing I was ever expecting, especially from her uptight ass. She thinks she's a motherfuckin' saint but then goes and pulls that sort of shit. Took everything I had not to hold her down and thrust my cock in her."

"I bet, shit. Cherry ever pulled that sort; I'd have her tied to my bed. I'd fuck her till she couldn't sit down for the rest of the day." He slaps my shoulder and gives it a brotherly squeeze. "You better drink a few more of those. Maybe whiskey dick will help you out."

"Never thought I'd see the day I'd be asking for whiskey dick."

He chuckles. "Good luck, brother."

"You out of here?"

He nods. "I'm meeting Ares. Sinner set up another ammo order for us."

"Why's our VP picking it up and not one of us?" Odin's the youngest in our club and a damn good vice president.

"I heard he's got a new Doberman; I want to check it out." He shrugs, and I relax a bit.

A laugh breaks free, finally a reason for me to smile today. "You guys and those damn dogs."

He shrugs unperturbed. "The ol' ladies have been trying to get the resources together to start a rescue. Figure if I'm building Cherry a house, I may as well get a dog to go with it."

"Jesus, settling down, huh?"

"One day, it'll be you, brother."

Smirking, I shake my head. "I won't hold my breath. You taking the truck, then?"

He nods. "I'll catch you later."

"Bet." We bump knuckles, and then he's out the door.

I'm left to my whiskey, which I promptly down again and gesture to Frost for some more. I'm not going to get much done today if I proceed with this routine.

A throat clears, garnering my attention. I glance back to find my blood cousin and MC brother, Viking, behind me.

"'Sup, man," I greet.

He grunts and takes the seat beside me. Vike's brooding will give mine a run for the money any day. He motions to Frost, and the prospect quickly hands over a cold bottled water to the Oath Keepers' prez. Everyone is well aware of our prez remaining sober for the most part. He likes to keep his head straight, and I respect him for it. When Viking goes off the deep end, there's no reeling him back, and I don't think any of us could handle seeing him treat Princess poorly like he did for a beat.

"Odin just split."

He nods and grunts. "Asshole stopped by my office. Mentioned a dog."

With a smirk, I nod back. Regardless of him and Odin being blood brothers, he doesn't treat him any different than the other members around here. Hell, Viking's been more of a father figure to him than Jekyll ever was. *May that man rot in the fiery pits of hell.* "Any updates on when we're headed out?" I go for a subject change, not wanting to think about Jekyll any longer.

"We're riding tomorrow night. I'll be letting the others know tomorrow at noon. They'll have enough time to reel everyone in on lock-down, and then we'll take care of business. I don't want it discussed until then."

"Damn." My fingers massage my temples. I still have my principal to think about, and dare I say it, but worry over.

"What's going on?" He grumbles after chugging half his bottle. The plastic flexes, making a crunching sound in his mammoth grip.

"It's Amelia."

"Who?" His face screws up, not familiar with her name.

"The principal, she's in my room. I don't know what to do with her while we're gone, either."

Frost belches loudly, and Viking casts him an unamused glance before replying. "The motherfucker is next to glasses and chips. Needs to shut his fuckin' trap."

I agree. That's fucking gross.

"Torch won't let her get away," he rationalizes, and it doesn't bring me any relief.

"Shit, man. I'll come back, and he'll have strangled her something."

He chuckles lowly. "Sounds like problem solved then."

I shake my head. "I promised not to hurt her."

He snorts.

I roll my eyes. "I'm serious."

"Yeah? Now I'm curious what this bitch looks like. She must be fine as fuck if you've switched from tormentor to tormented."

"Fuck off."

His eyes light up. I pretty much just confirmed whatever he'd had in his head. *Fuck my life.* The last thing any of these assholes around here need is leverage to give me any more shit. We bust each other's balls enough without any extra ammunition readily available to dip into. "Mm."

"Nah, it's not like that."

He nods, completely not buying it.

"I just don't want her to end up six feet under or traumatized is all."

"See if Princess and Bethany will check on her and bring her a sandwich every now and then. I wouldn't let Smokey's old ass in there, though. He may drug her and attempt to get his dick hard."

"And I'll castrate the old perverted fuck," I mutter.

Vike's brows raise. "Damn, brother. She gonna be on the back of your bike soon? Honey will pitch a fit, that I'm sure of."

I shrug. "She won't, and Honey's well aware that she's only a means to an end. Nothing more."

"Ask the other brothers who're wifed up. They'll tell you what a jealous bitch Honey can be when a new ol' lady comes around."

"She's not my ol' lady. There are too many women out there that I still need to fuck."

He smirks, done arguing about it. "I'll take your word on it, brother. Talk to P and Bethany."

"Bet, that sounds like a good plan."

"And don't say shit to that uptight bitch about anything, or I'll have Torch cut your fuckin' tongue out."

I scoff and take a gulp of the whiskey. It burns a bit but helps make my thoughts of Amelia a bit less prominent. "My lips are sealed. Honey's, however, need to be wrapped around my cock, especially if we're popping smoke tomorrow. I'm gonna go hunt her ass down and remind her she belongs on her knees with me."

Viking quietly chuckles, shaking his head. He fist bumps my knuckles as I stand and head in the opposite direction. I set out for Honey but end up in the kitchen. I need to make something for Amelia. I don't want her getting hungry or wanting for anything while she's with me. Honey can always suck my dick later. There's no rush to get to her.

"Her name's Princess? Is that her actual name or a nickname?" Amelia asks me the following day. I've been telling her about P and Bethany *captivesitting* her while I'm on our run. "And it'll just be her and a dark-haired woman? Are you leaving?"

With a huff, I get defensive. "You're not supposed to be asking questions, remember? And it's none of your business what I'll be doing. I told you already, I have to work so the women will be checking in on you and making sure you have food."

"Are they good people, though?"

"Am I?" I can't help but ask, miffed at the tone of her inquisitiveness. "And you've met P already, she helped you shower."

She blushes for some reason and doesn't say anything else regarding Princess.

"If an old fucker comes in here smelling like smoke, you kick him in the nuts. Don't hesitate, just nail him good and hard, straight away." Smokey's always been a pervert. I don't think he'll try anything, but better safe than sorry.

Her eyes widen. "What? Why on earth would I kick an old man? I'm not a violent woman!"

"He's a pervert. My prez said the old fucker may drug you and try to fuck ya. I won't be in here to snap his neck for you."

Her lip trembles and I have to hold back my laugh. She's not as hard now with all those suppressants leaving her system. She's starting to act like a normal woman. It's refreshing and beyond sexy. Just being in her presence has me strung tight. I want to sink my cock inside her so badly; it kept me up half the goddamn night. I've been jerking my cock enough with her here that I outta have bigger forearms in no time.

"Don't get upset...I'm telling you how it is. Be a good girl and listen to me."

She glares, her temper flaring up. I love it that she's mouthy and feisty as fuck. Makes my dick harder than granite. "Don't patronize me," she hisses, and I flash her a predatory grin.

"I'll do whatever the fuck I want. You best not forget that. Besides, I wasn't. I was telling you to fucking do as I said, just trying to be nice about it." I shrug, and she sighs. "What now?"

She stares at the floor and admits softly, "I want to go home."

"All this because I won't be around for a few days? You're going to miss me? I thought you hated me?"

"I don't necessarily hate you, although I should, you *did* kidnap me. And to answer your questions, no, I won't miss you."

"But? I can hear there's a but coming."

"But, in here, you're what I know."

"Ah. So, it's not me you'll miss, it's fear of the unknown that has your feathers ruffled."

She shrugs, not replying. Amelia's finally opening up to me, even just a little bit, and I have to go take care of business. Figures. I knew she wouldn't be able to hold out on me for too long though. We'll just have to pick back up where we left off when I return. She's got two weeks of vacation, so I'll have another week before the school will begin to notice her absence when I return. I've made progress with her this past week; I know I can get even further with some more time. This ride is coming up at the shittiest time.

"Look at me," I command, and her gaze hits my chin. "My eyes," I snap. She complies, and I tell her seriously, "Princess and Bethany won't let anything happen to you. I won't be far, just taking care of some work. I'll be back before you know it, and everything will be okay."

She stays quiet, and I give her a sincere look.

"Have I broken my word to you this far?"

She shakes her head.

"So, trust me when I say you'll be okay. As long as you're in my room, you're safer here than in a police office."

"If I had to guess, I'd say everyone here is extremely dangerous too. Your idea of safe and mine are clearly on opposite spectrums."

"If anyone hurts you, I'll kill them myself. That's one promise you can count on."

She doesn't want to admit it, but I can see the relief in her eyes. Surprisingly, I really do mean my promise. If someone so much as fucks with her, it'll be hell to pay, 'cause I'll be on the warpath in her name.

Amelia

"Hey, girl, how you holding up?" The striking blonde from before greets. This time around, I don't have a gag in my mouth and can respond with words.

"As well as I can be, I suppose, given my circumstances."

She sends me a weird look. "I wanted to stop by and bring you a slice of lasagna. Did Blaze leave you any snacks?"

I shake my head.

"Ugh, that man is clueless sometimes. Guys don't realize that if we're going to be cooped up all day, doing nothing, we at least need some good munchies and Netflix."

"I didn't think this was a vacation, with the ropes and all," I mutter snarkily. I expect her to cop an attitude in response, but she bursts out with a surprised laugh instead. She turns to the doorway and says, "See, I knew she had to be different if Blaze was unsure of what to do with her."

"No kidding." A dark-haired woman about the same height as Princess steps into the room, and I can see who the voice belongs to. She sends me a curious look, and I return it with my own. They don't appear to be too much younger than me, and they're in yoga pants and T-shirts, so I'm going to go out on a limb and guess that they aren't part of the club whores.

"Bethany, this is Amelia. She's the principal who's been giving Maverick anxiety."

I pale. Stuck in ropes, surrounded by bikers, including their women, and I'm clearly not their favorite person around here. I've met Maverick's father before when I've had to call for him to be picked up. I've never met his mother though, as she's always working when I call. Annabelle Teague is another. I've met her father but never her mother.

"Ah, Maverick," I note. "It's nice to finally meet you."

"Not sure how nice it'll be if you keep giving my kid grief. I've decked bitches for less."

Princess grins and nods. "She really has. It's pretty entertaining."

My stare meets hers. "And you're Princess, I guess?" I question.

Her smile grows. "My brother was talking about me?"

I nod, chalking it up to them being siblings after all. Maybe that's her role around here, being his sister that helps him take care of whatever he needs. I don't think I could get on board with this sort of thing if I had a brother who was a gang member.

"He said your name is Princess, and he seems fond of you."

"Aww, that little dickface," she coos and Bethany snorts.

"Dickface sums it up," she agrees, and I nod as well.

Princess giggles. "See, B? I like her, she's got lady balls."

Bethany shrugs. "Not sure she'd fit in very well, though. From what I hear, she has a huge stick stuck up her ass."

"I'm right here." I raise my hand and wave. "Also, I'm pretty sure there's no stick in there."

"We'll see, I reckon." She shrugs. I seem to have Princess's approval, but this one's going to be a little more difficult to get on her good side. Understandable since I've suspended her son in the past. In my defense, he shouldn't be kissing girls, it's against school policy. Any type of sexual misconduct is not tolerated, period. He's starting early on the road of sexual harassment, and I won't stand for it.

"I'm not that bad, really. I just have to do my job."

"Look, lady, I don't care what you 'have' to do. You be a bitch to my kid again, and I'm flattening your pretty face."

I remain quiet but shake my head. I'll never understand women like her, who are violent and justify it with nonsense.

"Let's discuss that later," Princess cuts in. "Right now, you need something to eat. You can throw a munch on some pasta, and we'll come check on you later."

I agree and ask, "He's really not coming back anytime soon?" It seriously bothers me, knowing Blaze isn't around. I don't know why, but the man is building some trust inside me.

Her head tilts, and she stares me down for a beat. "You like him."

I shake my head.

"I call bullshit. It has to be unbearably boring in here, though, and you just gave me an idea."

"I did?"

She nods, tossing a glance at Bethany. "Mav's busy, right?"

"Yeah, why?"

"Let's grab some cards and play *Bullshit.*" She grins. She must win a lot to be this eager.

"I'm down, but the prissy bitch won't cuss," her friend concedes.

"Wanna bet?" Princess retorts, and I cut in.

"I don't know how to play."

"No worries, we can teach you."

My shoulders bounce, and my chest doesn't feel as tight anymore at the thought of being left alone. "Sounds good to me."

"Great. We'll give you some time to eat while we round up enough cards and see if a few of the other ladies want in."

My eyes grow wide. "Is that allowed?" I ask on a whisper.

She waves me off. "Shit, girl, who's going to stop me? I'm the prez's ol' lady; I do whatever the hell I want."

Still wide-eyed, I nod, growing excited to get the chance to meet more people here. Hopefully they don't hate me like Bethany is on the verge of. Regardless, it'll be better than sitting here and staring at the wall. I've tried to think of every way possible to escape, but it's fruitless when there aren't any windows. This will at least help the time pass.

Blaze

The ride's long. Viking had us leave at night. Riding in the dark is a blessing and a curse. There aren't too many cages on the road, but you have to be vigilant where wild animals are concerned. The cops usually leave you be, too, unless you run across a bored officer who wants to stir shit up. We can't have any of that on this run, considering we're strapped like we're going off to war. 2 Piece, from the other charter, is following us in a truck loaded down with a shit ton of ammo and supplies. Viking wants us to hit the cartel hard, and ASAP, to draw some of the heat off border patrol. If we can take out a few of their cells, then ICE and border patrol can use more of their sources on cutting down the illegal border jumpers. The sex trafficking and drugs entering our country have amped up significantly. No one knows that, though, since the media won't report on it. They're too busy running with their own agendas.

We were briefed loading up, and Vike's contact said twenty American soldiers were just slaughtered right outside our border, but no one's reporting on that important story either. He said that the government is looking into hiring private mercenaries to help drive down the violence toward Americans. We're mainly concerned about Texas, but them heading in from other states can be an issue. If it's not taken care of swiftly, they can get farther into the states, and those places will see a spike in crimes. Poor people entering illegally will do anything they can to survive. I know that firsthand with the way we grew up with Jekyll. If only more people understood the true impact it has on our country, they'd be more apt in stopping it rather than promoting it.

After hearing Nightmare's story about him getting attacked by the lions, I'm a little apprehensive about what we'll find. I'm down to help out, but I don't want to get attacked by a lion or any other wild fucking exotic animal. Another thing been riding on my mind is Doctor Amelia Stone. The bitch has been driving me crazy. I'm confident with women; they love me...but she's an enigma. She seems to have no interest in me at all, then she rubs her pussy all over my fingers when she thinks I'm asleep. What the fuck am I supposed to do with that?

I'm a man. I have my limits just like everyone else. When she did that, it took everything in me to hold back from having her. Hell, she wouldn't know what hit her if I did make a move. I can't, though. I promised not to, and I'm a man of my word. I may not be the best guy around, but that's one thing I stick to.

"We're close, brothers," Viking grumbles to the group when we pull into the lot of an old motel. He distracts me from the path my thoughts were going down, and I pay better attention to my surroundings. He continues, "It's ten a.m. now. We're meeting up with the Nomads at seven p.m. Get some shut-eye and grub, then be ready to talk some business. We have a general plan in mind, and we'll discuss it all when everyone's rested and together."

We nod our agreement and head for the front office. The old lady doesn't bat an eye at us. I'm guessing this must be a frequent stay for the Nomads when they're passing through. It must be why the prez stopped here. I hand over my thirty bucks, collect my room key and wheel my hog in the room with me. Ain't no sheisty motherfucker jacking my shit while I'm passed the fuck out. I give the brothers around me a chin-lift on my way in and then position my bike across the door once it's closed and locked. Just in case anyone tries kicking the door in while I'm sleeping, I'll have a beat of a warning. You never know what kind of assholes are hanging around these tiny towns bordering Mexico.

I take a quick, lukewarm shower to rinse off the road grime and hit the sack. Another thing about these shit holes is that they never have good hot water heaters, so you get used to taking cold showers. Leaving the compound at two a.m. to ride all night had me working to keep my eyes peeled. It's another thing entirely when you're up, partying and dancing or whatever with a ton of people around. When it's just the wind and the roar of our engines, it'll attempt to lull you to sleep. I had heavy metal blasting in my helmet just to try and keep focused. A quick nod off on a motorcycle can end your life depending on your surroundings and your speed.

I send P a text, checking on my girl. I can send one tonight again before we bounce out of this shit hole, but then it's river city. No tech allowed while we're on these sorts of runs except for our comm devices. You never know who's watching and may be keeping track.

The Nomads got in good with a contact years back, and it's worked to our benefit. It pays to have a few contacts in high places when your club tends to break the law. We've learned through experience and have gotten smarter, so for the most part, we stay out of the cops' path more often than not.

After hearing Princess reassure me that Amelia's straight and the ol' ladies played some cards with her while I was passed out, I can relax a bit where she's concerned. I'm shocked Princess replied right away, but then again, she was probably waiting for her ol' man to check in with her too. Knowing Viking, hard ass and all, he'd have called her as soon as he plugged his phone in this morning when we'd arrived. I can't blame him; I'd do the same if I were in his shoes. Hell, I'm not even close with Amelia, and I was checking up on the woman as soon as I woke up.

I move my bike out of the way and crack my door open, popping my head out. Nightmare and Saint are both there, smoking cigarettes. I head outside, clad in jeans, bandana, and white socks. Fuck what anyone thinks, I just got up. "Hey bro, can I bum one?" I gesture to his pack. They're all crushed on one end. He probably had them shoved in his pocket.

Night nods and holds the pack out to me.

I don't generally smoke, but this is the first run of this nature that I've been on in years. I need the nicotine to chill my nerves the fuck out. Saint will snort a bit of powder for this shit. I don't understand how that fucker functions so hyped up. I need a joint or something to calm me the fuck down. "You smoking again?" I ask. "Thought your ol' lady put an end to that shit, brother."

Saint passes over a lighter, grinning like a fool. *Crazy pretty boy motherfucker.*

Night mutters, "She's not the boss of me."

I snort, and Saint laughs outright. Nightmare's so fucking pussy whipped it's not even funny. He and Viking are two peas in a pod with their bitches. They're obsessed and even fuck their women together from what I hear.

He shrugs it off. "She bought me the pack, knew what Mexico does to me."

"Smart woman," I retort.

"Nah shit," he grumbles.

If I had to guess, he's as stressed as I am and probably hangry. "You guys grab anything to eat yet?"

"I could go for some pussy, but Jude would cut my dick off. She already threatened before I left."

I raise a brow, and he smiles maniacally in return. Of course, he'd take a good, secluded chick and turn her into a goddamn psychopath. "I was thinking food, brother."

Nightmare replies, "I was gonna hit up the diner next door."

"Bet, I'll head over with you. I'm fucking starving."

I quickly grab a white T-shirt and my boots, already picturing the club sandwich and fries I plan on ordering. Saint falls in step with us, commenting, "Only two more hours, brothers. Then it's showtime." He rubs his hands together with excitement.

Nightmare and I don't say anything in return. Like either of us needed the reminder. I'm sure we're both watching the clock today.

Heathen

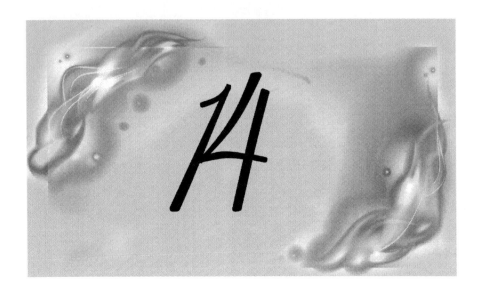

Amelia

"Hey, I brought you breakfast," Princess offers as she enters Blaze's room the following day. I'd been up for a while, used to being on a strict school schedule for so many years. With Blaze in the bed, I seem to sleep longer than usual. I thought it was the aftermath of being drugged, but maybe it's just him and his presence beside me.

"Thank you."

"How are you feeling today?"

I shake my head, sighing. "I can't remember the last time I drank more than a few glasses of wine."

She laughs. "I told you, I can make some bomb ass margaritas. They go hand in hand with playing cards."

"These men don't care if you drink like that?"

She shrugs and takes a seat in Blaze's big chair after setting the plate of food beside me. "It wasn't a big deal yesterday since the club was busy riding. I won't be getting that carried away again until they come home, though. I need to be ready in case anyone needs something."

"Blaze said he had to work. Does that mean you're in charge? What's his place here?"

"I'm not in charge, no." She giggles. "This is an MC club for men, but I am the president's ol' lady, so a sense of responsibility does fall to me. Especially when they have a job to do or whatever. They don't tell me much as far as that's concerned."

"That sounds like a lot resting on your shoulders—a lot of responsibility."

She waves it off, relaxing back and crossing her legs. "It's the life I know, the life I love," she concedes. "As for Blaze...I'm not sure what exactly I should tell you about him."

"Anything, please. I don't think he's planning on letting me go anytime soon, so any information about the man would help."

She nods. "Hmm, I probably shouldn't. After being around you the past few days, you're actually not that bad, though. At least not what I was expecting, anyhow. If only you'd change your perspective on the club and the members, maybe things could be different. Anyhow, Blaze..." She trails off and taps her chin, clearly thinking of what to share with me. I am the enemy here, after all.

"Well, I can't talk about club stuff, it's against the code. I can let you know that he's my husband's cousin and a good friend of mine. He's a vital member of this club and an officer. He had a really rough life growing up...umm, what else? Well, he's made some serious changes on how he treats women, and he's been my personal protector since he showed up here, years back. This is all stuff you could find out just by hanging around here."

"Wait, he protects you?" I butt in, unable to hold my building curiosity.

She offers a wide smile, not put off in the slightest by my inquisitiveness. "He nearly died to protect me. That was one of the worst days of my life, and he stood in front of me and took a serious beating from a rival club. They cut him up pretty badly and even shot him. He managed to pick off as many guys as he could before they got to Bethany and me. It was a dark day. He's stuck to my side like glue. This job they're on now is the first time he's not stayed back with me."

"Wow," I breathe, conjuring the image of him being brutally injured and not enjoying the feelings it gives me in my gut.

"He's been through some serious stuff, for sure. He wasn't always a good man. He was probably worse than you can ever imagine, but all of that's changed. He may come off as cocky to you, but that's because he's a Casanova around here. The ladies absolutely love him. He makes us laugh a lot, and if you ever see the man dance..." She whistles low.

My brows raise, and she grins. "Dance?"

"Yep, when Blaze parties and gets some liquor in his system, he ends up on the bar top, shirtless, abs on display, dancing like he's straight out of *Magic Mike*." She giggles again, and I smile. I wasn't planning on watching something of that nature, but when it was on TV, my curiosity won me over. I may've watched some of it and understand her reference.

"I clearly don't know him, it sounds like," I mention, and she shakes her head, agreeing with my statement.

"I wish you got to meet him under different circumstances. You'd have a different opinion of him for sure."

"It's hard for me to think like that when he drugged and kidnapped me. He's holding me here with threats of disposing my body if I misbehave."

She shrugs as if it's nothing. "We all do shit we're not proud of. Have you ever considered that maybe it wasn't his choice?"

"You mean like he was following someone else's orders?" I ask, and she nods. "No...I just assumed..."

"Exactly. You assumed. But in your defense, you didn't know any better. Now, you do."

"You're saying that it wasn't his idea, that he did what he was told to by someone else."

She stares into my eyes and seriously answers, "I'm not saying anything. Just think of things differently." She winks, and my mind is exploding with a burst of new thoughts and scenarios. Could Blaze be innocent in all of this? Well, as guiltless as possible? He's clearly still at fault for executing the order, but her comment has my mind spinning.

I upset the club, so they sent in someone to deal with me. Blaze is just doing what he's told. If I think of it as a job, it makes sense. Granted, it's not the same thing, but it helps me understand him a little better.

"Thank you, Princess," I say, truly grateful for the small kernel of information she's offered.

She beams. "Now, eat up. I'll grab you another robe, so you have something clean to wear after you shower."

She made me promise yesterday before the ol' ladies came into the room that I wouldn't tell Blaze if she let me borrow a robe. She didn't think it would be comfortable for me to be naked while surrounded by other women, playing cards. I'd never been so grateful for a piece of clothing before. It may've only been a thin robe, but it gave me a shred of my dignity back.

"Yes, ma'am." I grab the muffin she offers and take a decent-sized bite.

I met Cherry yesterday, and she was telling me all about her baking. I'm betting these are from her. She's talented. I savor each bite as the muffin's flavors are like a burst of sweetness as I chew. Last week I'd never have grabbed for a muffin, but here, you take what you can get I've quickly learned. It's been an adjustment for my stomach, for sure, but I've also been secretly enjoying the carb overload I'd never allow myself to have outside of here.

Princess sticks out her tongue, being silly at my *ma'am* comment and hands over a bottle of orange juice with the lid off. I'm still tied to this long rope that reaches across the room, so normal things like twisting my wrists to remove a lid is still a difficult task.

I hand the juice back to her, and she sets it on Blaze's dresser before leaving to grab me a clean robe. Maybe I'll get lucky, and she'll eventually bring me some yoga pants or something as well.

I'd tried to explore Blaze's drawers when he initially put me on this rope leash thing, and I was finally able to walk around, but they didn't hold anything interesting. I figured being a guy, he'd have a pocketknife stashed somewhere or some other small weapon type gadget that I could use to assist in getting me free, but there was nothing. His dresser is surprisingly tidy too. The bottom drawer was loaded down with mechanic and travel magazines. I'll admit, I was shocked to see that he reads. I know that's biased, but it is what it is. I judged him, but clearly, he's judged me as well. The other drawers are neatly stuffed with underwear, socks, and white undershirts.

I wanted to toss a shirt on but held back for multiple reasons. For one, I can't get it on while my hands are tied. With the robes, Princess used the sash to tie around my boobs, so it sort of drapes over me like a short, silky dress. The other reason was because of his warnings. I don't want to anger him and make him treat me worse, from not following his directions of staying naked. I took the robe more than willingly because it was offered by someone he trusts. I wanted to slide a pair of his underwear on too but couldn't get over the thoughts of how many women he's slept with and if he's ever bleached them. If there was a washer and dryer in here, I'd do it myself, but his room's sparse.

The bathroom isn't much of an improvement, either. The man is a minimalist. Under the sink, he has more soap and shampoo, which smells far too good. He has some deodorant, body spray, hair gel, detangler, toothpaste, and his toothbrush. I don't know if he hid the razors before bringing me here or what, but I haven't seen anything sharp since arriving.

His room is almost too clean if I'm being honest. Did he tidy it up before I got here? Or rather, did someone else clean it? He doesn't strike me as the type to clean anything. If what Princess says is true, I have no idea what he's really like outside of being my kidnapper.

She's back in a flash, helping me out of yesterday's robe and into the shower. The position's awkward, though, my rope doesn't reach far enough for me to really get under the spray. After fighting with it, I finally huff and hang my head in defeat. I can't believe I'm in this position in the first place. I was an idiot to ever think I was safe. I hate to admit it, but Blaze is right. If times were different or something happened, I'd need him to protect me. That thought drives me crazy inside for some reason. I hate needing anyone, and especially a man. I'm independent. I always have been, but he's opening my eyes to other possibilities. Sure, people have spewed things in the past, but I never stopped to listen. With him, I have no other choice but to hear him out.

Looking at the circumstances I'm in now, would I be here if I'd had a smart, strong husband to help protect me? Probably not, and that's a big pill to swallow. At the very least, that alpha would be losing his mind right now over trying to find me. As it stands, I have no one looking for or missing me. That's a hard reality to grasp.

This is Blaze's fault. He's kept me here, made me ridiculously vulnerable, and it's making me think things, like finding a man when I get out of here. If I ever do, how do I find one who is big and strong like Blaze, who I could possibly put up with and not want to toss my drink in his face at every meal? Blaze is a brash and headstrong man, but I've quickly learned he's also very intelligent. He's rough around the edges, but he also feeds me and keeps me warm. It's reducing things to the basic nature and what science often attempts to prove about women and men being on an animal level with one another.

Princess uses a big cup to get me wet enough and runs her hands caked in soap over my body. She kneads my back, shoulders, neck, and head. It feels divine, and I'm understanding more each day why the president of the MC married her. She's a great caretaker, even I can see that. "Do you have kids?" I ask out of the blue, and she pauses.

"No. Maybe someday." She answers quickly and pours water to rinse me off. There's no lingering touches and orgasms like the previous shower. I was a little apprehensive getting in here, but also a tad excited at the thought of her touch. It's on the forbidden side, and I'm stunned that I enjoyed it so much.

"Why are you with the president if you like women?"

She snorts out a giggle. "Women aren't my main interest. Besides, Viking wouldn't take no for an answer."

I spin around, eyes wide, "D-did he kidnap you too? Or force you?"

She rolls her eyes. "Our story is between him and me. I will say it was crazy and fast, but I'd never want another man. He proved to me that no other man would ever satisfy me the way he does." She pauses and then smiles softly. Her head tilts as she says, "I'm going to divulge one thing, but don't you dare judge him on it."

My brows raise. "I'll try not to, I promise."

She nods. "I don't know why I care what you think, but I don't want you to have a bad opinion of him because of it. My ol' man has his reasons why he does the crazy stuff he does."

I nod, intrigued.

"He found a rival of the clubs trying to hurt me. I was all alone, fighting, and Viking helped me."

I smile. "Why would I ever judge him wrongly on that? He did the right thing."

She agrees. "He killed him for touching me."

I gasp because that's just plain crazy.

Her brow furrows, and she steps out of the tub. She reaches for the towel. "You promised. You can't jump to conclusions. Around here, you don't know the whole story behind things. Try to remember that."

I swallow, my voice wanting to come out as a croak. These men kill, and she just reminded me. It's easier to try and forget those savage parts, to pretend like things around here aren't so serious. It's been helping me cope, but it's not reality. "How can you love him, knowing he's killed someone?"

She shrugs. "He's killed many people. That doesn't determine whether I love him or not. How he treats me, how he makes me feel...that's how I love him. I won't lie to you, his killing doesn't bother me, not like it should. Maybe I'm broken inside?" She implies it as a question, but I don't think she truly believes that. I think she's a product of her environment. Being around such acts can shape a person and determine their norm.

For me, it's outrageous and alarming. Has Blaze really killed people as well? If so, how many and why? When you strip away his cocky attitude he carries during the day, and it leaves the warm comfort of him at nighttime, it's hard for me to picture him as a ruthless killer. I could be wrong about it like Princess implied that I don't know the full intent of each person around here. I don't think I am though. I believe Blaze has killed people in the past. The scariest part of that revelation? I still want to see him; it hasn't shunned me away completely like it would've prior to being kidnapped.

Is this the beginning of Stockholm Syndrome? "Shit."

"Whoa, did you just curse? And not while playing Bullshit?" Princess gawks, drawing my attention back to her and the robe she's busily tying around me.

"Uh, did I say that out loud?"

She nods, gazing at me curiously. "I haven't heard you swear before. Well, aside from the Bullshit game, anyhow," I swallow tightly again, my chest feeling hot.

"It's because I don't curse." I slam my eyes closed, cringing at the revelations. "I have to get out of this place..." I whisper, knowing that I'm already beginning to change.

Blaze

I embrace each of our Nomad brothers as we all crowd into a secluded area. We'd rode down I-10 for a beat before Viking had us turn off at an old dilapidated adobe house—what remains of it, anyhow. It's not easy to tell what it was without being up close. Half of the place is falling down, and it's about the size of a shack. Hard to imagine someone or multiple people once lived in this tiny shit hole. There's a dirt road that runs alongside it, the path carrying on as far as my eyes can see.

"Where the fuck are we, bro?" I ask Ruger. He's a Nomad who I instantly clicked with when the Widow Makers merged with the Oath Keepers, and I was patched over into the hybrid charter. Viking used to ride with the Nomads before the shit hit the fan, and we patched over to form the hybrid Oath Keeper charter.

He exhales and digs out a flask. It's probably full of moonshine. Chaos has the Nomads hooked on the shit. "Out in bum fuck Egypt, brother."

"You been riding on that dirt death trap for long?" I ask, referring to the rocky dirt road they'd come from. The same one that doesn't seem to ever end.

He nods. "That ride is slow, long, and fucking stupid." He uses his bandana in an attempt to wipe away some dust from his face. With his dark hair and scruff, he looks like a hajji. All of the Nomads are heavily caked in the shit. It looks like they're a bunch of dirtbags. I suppose it'll help them blend in, though.

I chuckle to myself at the reference.

He sips from his flask and continues, "But it's our way in. The tiny border patrol station there allows us to make our runs and doesn't see shit as far as weapons and ammunition are concerned. Good bunch of guys stuck in that spot. Frankly, I think they're just grateful to have some sort of backup occasionally in BFE. Can't say I blame 'em either."

"Bet." I nod, my relief written all over my expression. I wasn't looking forward to possibly getting popped and doing time since I'm strapped the fuck down with various weapons. I would do time for my club, but it doesn't mean I want to.

"Brothers," Exterminator interrupts. He's the longest riding Nomad out of their group. Viking, Nightmare, Saint, and Sinner were all a part of their little group until Vike set down his roots. "The road ahead is bumpy as fuck. We've gotta take it slow, so it'll feel like it takes for fucking ever. We've got a spot set up on the other side where you can sleep and eat. Watch for coyotes, and if border patrol stops us, don't pull any weapons. If a Mexican cop stops us, shoot first and ask questions later. Any cops that stop us are on the cartel's payroll and were sent to kill us. They make their money from promising illegals passage for payment, then they kill them."

Various grumbles ring out, and I'm thinking the same damn thing. This situation is fucked.

Spider speaks up. "It's a shitastic condition, but it's not why we're here. We're headed into Mexico to deal with the cartel. We have various cells we've been tracking with the approval of our government ties, but there's not enough of us. We need to hit the cartel like we did with the Iron Fists. If we take them out one at a time, they'll either overtake us or else get away before we have a chance to move on their location."

Mercenary interrupts. "When in the fuck did we start doing shit for the government?" He's salty as fuck because the cops where he's from hate his troublemaking ass. I would too if I were them. Merc stirs up all kinds of shit. Vike had to hand him his ass when he first showed up. Our prez doesn't put up with any bullshit.

Viking glares at the newest member. "We're being paid, and our club's being left the fuck alone. You gonna cry like a bitch, then take your ass back home and make some fucking sandwiches."

Mercenary growls then shuts the fuck up. He doesn't want to push the prez too far, or else he'll end up with an ass beating like he's never experienced. That'll be the end of it, though. We handle our issues swiftly and effectively, but I don't envy the brother on the other side of Viking's temper.

Exterminator continues. "We'll pick back up when we get to our spot. We have some images of key players to pass around. We'll be paid much more if we can come home with a few of those fuck sticks alive. Either way, we have a job to do, and I've already made it crystal fucking clear that our lives come before any sniveling motherfucker."

Viking nods and orders, "Let's fucking ride." The roar of our engines shakes the ground, and our group pushes forward.

My ass is chapped and sore by the time we get into Mexico and are able to stop again. I've got dust and grime in places it shouldn't be, and I'm pretty sure I smell like a dog. Asphalt, dirt, exhaust, sweat, and Mexico will do that to you. It's been too long since I've been on a decent length run, and aside from the dirt road, I've missed it more than I realized. There's something freeing about riding and just zoning out in the wind.

I wonder if Amelia's been on a bike. Nah, she's far too snooty for it. She wouldn't wrinkle her business suit or want her hair jacked up. It'd be a task for her to pull the stick out of her ass and just enjoy it. However, there's no doubt in my mind she'd look fine as fuck if she did. I can imagine her all leathered up, with her perky tits and nose stuck up in the air.

Mm...makes my cock hard, just thinking of it—and now's not the time for that shit. Although tapping some Mexican pussy down here may help me relieve some stress, it's not as good as the real thing. I guess we'll see if we have any time for it or not. Viking already made it clear we're here to shoot some motherfuckers, not get our dicks wet.

I'm peeling a bandana from my face as Sinner hands me a couple of photos. I flip through them as he mutters, "These are the fuckers we take alive if we have the chance. I'm down for the extra payday, but I'd rather put a bullet in their heads and get back to June." He shrugs, and I can't help but agree.

I don't have an ol' lady like most of the brothers, but I have Amelia to think about until I break her down some. Once she's calmed the fuck down and agrees to back off the club, then I'll be done with her. I think so, anyhow. There's a sick twisted part of me that hopes she really fights me on it, so I have a reason to fuck with her more. I shouldn't want to torment her, but something inside me craves it. I think it's the fact that she seems oblivious to me like I don't affect her at all. That shit's been driving me crazy. I couldn't stop thinking of it on the way here. It's probably what kept me from passing the fuck out on the road.

If it weren't for this cartel shit going down, Viking would be on my ass over the principal. I guess this ride is a blessing and a curse. It gives me an excuse to spend more time with her. That's probably a bad thing, but fuck it. You only live once, right? My life hasn't been something to write home about, so I may as well do whatever the fuck intrigues me. Right now, it's that stubborn woman tied up in my room.

"I hear you, man," I reply and pass the stack of photos over to Chaos.

He shuffles through them with an exhale. Clearly, he's got something on his mind, too, and it isn't Mexico.

"You straight, brother?" I ask. I've bartended a lot in the past, so it's made me fairly close to all the brothers. They've confided in me at some point about random stuff, so I can't help but ask Chaos what's up with him. If I hadn't talked to them in the past about personal matters, I'd keep my mouth shut.

He meets my eyes, his expression seemingly exhausted. "Just been worrying about my girl. She's due any day now, and this pregnancy has been rougher than the last. I'm worried I'll be in the middle of a fucking shoot-out and miss her going into labor. I want to be on a flight ASAP to Foxboro when I get the call."

I nod. "I can imagine. Sorry to hear she's still having trouble carrying this one."

He rakes his hand through his hair and grins. "Guess the little guy is a big baby. Probably gonna be another football player in the family."

I grin back, glad to see him lighten up a bit. "Probably, brother, with you and her ol' man, your family is set up to be pro ballplayers for generations to come."

He agrees, being the proud poppa he is all the time. You'd never guess the big fucker used to play pro football and was super fucking famous. He went from being on the straight and narrow to joining a biker club and running moonshine. Crazy ass. He's also extremely protective of his daughter; her pregnancy seems to be no exception to that protection either.

We're interrupted by Exterminator, his deep gravelly voice growling with authority. "Spider has the maps on his cell. We'll be breaking off into small groups, and he'll send specific maps to each group. We ride at the same time, check in, and hit them at once. They'll have no time to react but to face us head-on. These shit holes are small, maybe five to ten men in each. You shoot straight, and you'll be riding home."

His words have us all silent, contemplative. This is important; we're helping our state, the border, and the government. Our actions here will save countless people in the future. This time around, they have to send in some bad men to take care of the evil. The Oath Keepers aren't good men, but we're not the same level of evil that the cartel has morphed into.

Spider finishes, "This won't take out the cartel by any means, but it'll disburse the small groups that our authorities are having trouble keeping up with. We help them out, we get paid, and they leave us the fuck alone. The downside is if the cartel catches wind of who the hit was from, there can be serious blowback. When we leave here, stick to the club and with your brothers when you can. We'll be riding home with you, just in case they try to strike back and you need backup."

Ares, the prez from the other Oath Keeper charter, speaks up. "We appreciate it. We have soldiers of the Russkaya Mafiya providing backup at home too. If the cartel comes to retaliate, they'll be at war with the Russians as well."

Viking steps forward. "I have Joker on call in Chicago. The Italian mafia has been made aware of the problem. They're keeping their hands out of it, but if the cartel pushes north, the Italians will push back. The cartel will be going to war with some of the most powerful families in the US." He drinks from his camelback and continues. "I have it on good authority that the Vendettis in New York are hoping the cartel moves in so they can declare war. Ruthless Vendetti wants more territory, and he's not writing off Mexico for that possible expansion."

Mercenary shakes his head, grumbling, "Fucking mafia, always wanting more."

We nod, knowing his statement is the truth. Those fuckers are never satisfied to just live with what they have.

Odin turns to the prez. "We have contacts in New York now?" It's understandable our VP would be questioning him, but Odin should already know this.

Viking shakes his head. "Not exactly. According to Joker, Dante the Devil Vendetti has been nominated to sit at the table of the five familias. Joker took the decision to the table to vote on, and the Devil informed him of Ruthless's plans to gain more territory if they intervene. You know those old Italian families, they won't do shit without gaining something in return."

"Fuck," Exterminator grumbles. "Let's get this shit over with. Viking, Spider, Ruger, and 2 Piece. Odin, Spin, Saint, and Knuckle Buster. Chaos, Twist, Sinner, and Magnum. Blaze, Nightmare, and Ares, you'll ride with me. Spider broke us up into these particular teams because each person contributes something that another doesn't have. Anyone have issues?"

We all shake our heads, willing to work with our brothers. We're well acquainted with each other, so it's not weird, more like getting to fuck some shit up with friends. Spider knows his stuff anyhow, so if he says we work the best together this way, then I'm going to take his word on it. Trusting the Nomads and the other charter took me a bit, but with time I was able to work it out. Viking wouldn't be so cool with them if it were any other way, and I spent most of my youth growing up with Vike. I trust his opinion.

Ares straps on Kevlar, and his club members follow suit. We all head over to the truck 2 Piece was stuck driving to dig out everything we need. The clubs have prepared for this well. There's Kevlar for everyone, weapons, and a shit ton of ammunition.

Twist straps on a handful of grenades flashing a pleased, manic looking grin. He was in the military, so I'm not surprised to see him reach for them. I, on the other hand, I'm staying far the fuck away from the grenades.

Spider holds his phone up as our burners begin vibrating. "I sent everyone the maps. If you click the app attached to it, it'll sync to your Bluetooth system installed in your helmet. I had to create a separate secured app instead of sending it through your bike's system."

Smart fucker. I wonder what Amelia would think of him. Jesus fuck. I can't be concerned with the mouthy woman right now, and I sure as fuck shouldn't care what she thinks about anyone. Still, though, I bet Spider would give her a run for her money in the smarts department. Make her educated ass question what she thinks she knows about the MC.

"Let's fuck some shit up; I'm ready." Nightmare growls in my direction, and I send him an answering nod. This is a personal vendetta for him, all stemming from the lion attack. The cartel fucked up with that one. Night will carry that shit to the grave. Not that I can blame him or anything. I'd be the same if I had to learn to ride all over again and walk normally. The guy couldn't even play the drums for a beat from what I hear. It fucked him up something fierce for a whole minute.

Ares's massive ass comes to a standstill next to me. He and 2 Piece clamp onto each other's wrists, each giving the other a serious look. Those two, along with Saint and Sinner, share their women, so it's more stressful on them, sending the other into war. They'd probably prefer it to be beside each other, but that could be a liability as well if they're too worried about their partner and not themselves.

2 Piece meets my stare next. "You got his back, brother?" he asks.

I chin-lift. "Always, man. He is my brother today and always."

2 Piece's expression relaxes just a touch at my proclamation. I know he needed to hear it. He glances at Ares again. "Ride safe."

"Bet." The oversized biker huffs. "You keep your ass the fuck outta gunfire." He grumbles something I can't hear, and 2 Piece heads for the back of the truck to help dig more shit out.

He turns to me. "He's still pissed the club voted for Cain to stay back." He shrugs. "Cain's ol' lady is knocked up. Of course, his ass needs to be home. I don't know a damn thing about labor and delivery. Cain is a veteran at it."

I nod. Although I have no idea about pregnancy or anything of the sort either. Our club brats are older, and the only time I see young kids is at Ares's charter. "I'm sure Princess is upset too. Damn near everyone she gives a fuck about is here," I mention, thinking of the stories I've heard.

There's been talk in the past of Princess and Ares being like siblings, and about him being the only MC member acceptable to marry her. That was according to her father. Supposedly Ares loved Princess fiercely, but the prez didn't realize those feelings were brotherly and not anything else. Clearly that changed with Viking in the picture, and I guess I sort of replaced his spot of an adopted brother when it comes to P.

"All right," Exterminator growls. "In and out, we meet back here and then ride as one. If someone has heat on 'em, I want them to be hit hard when they reach us all."

Viking swings his leg over his bike, ordering loudly, "Ride safe, brothers."

We all follow suit. My group consists of Nightmare, Ares, and Exterminator, so I'll follow Ex's direction. With my focus on him, I crank my engine. The lot thunders with our combined engines, then we're off in our separate directions, headed to fuck shit up.

Amelia

My days seem to merge into one after another. I'm beginning to wonder if Blaze is ever coming back. He said he had to do some work, but it's been days, it seems like. Did he leave town altogether? He hasn't returned at all, even to sleep. When he said he had things to take care of, I expected it to be the day or so. I'm not sure what to think anymore. I hope he doesn't leave me here for much longer.

The night he left had come and gone. I woke up, and the ol' ladies played cards and entertained me. I expected him to return later that afternoon, but nothing. Another day passed with Princess and Bethany keeping me company and again another night with me having the bed all to myself. You'd think that would be a wonderful thing, but without him and his body heat surrounding me, I've frozen and hardly gotten any sleep. I feel more exhausted than I did the day after he brought me here.

That's another thing. I don't know how long I've been here. Is it a week, or are we on week two at this point? Being drugged and secluded to a room has me scatterbrained and unable to distinguish what I should and shouldn't be feeling at this point. The scariest thought of all resting right under the surface is that I want him to come back. He implemented a sense of routine, and now it's all shaken up. I was learning what to expect with him each time he entered the room. With the women, I have no idea what to think.

"Hey, girl," Princess greets as she comes into Blaze's room. I won't lie, when I heard his door handle turn and the lock disengage, a piece of me hoped it was him. I wish I didn't feel that way. I hate him, after all, remember? Clearly not enough, if I'm looking forward to seeing his cocky grin pointed at seeing me looking like a complete mess.

She plops down on the bed beside me and offers me a soft smile. "Hi," I grumble, trying to rub my eyes. I'm exhausted, and I hate feeling this way.

"You didn't sleep well?"

I shake my head.

"I think I know of something that'll make you feel better."

My brow raises. "Mm?"

She nods. "Let's get you in the shower. I'm going to make you feel much better."

With a yawn, I nod and let her help me get up. She leads me into the bathroom, tugging along my rope leash. It's so demeaning, but I have to be grateful I'm able to move around somewhat freely at all. It's better than when I first arrived and was tied at my wrists and feet, and I could do nothing but lie around naked. In Princess's defense, she's allowed me to wear a silky robe since Blaze left, so there's that too.

"I have a surprise for you, sweetie."

"Uh-oh," I comment, and she giggles.

I've warmed up to her immensely over the time she's been spending to help take care of me. It helps that she's friendly, and I won't deny that she's gorgeous too. Everyone around here I've seen up to this point is far too attractive when a biker club comes to mind. I'd imagine big men with round bellies who stink and don't shower. Here, it's muscular dudes with confident attitudes and striking women, it's like the twilight zone or something. Several of the women are well educated and successful, I can only imagine what the men here hide or what it is they do to keep their significant others around.

"Let's start with us getting naked." She flashes me a flirty wink. I can't help but give her a smile of my own. This woman is crazy, but I'm doing what I need to, to make it out of here as soon as possible. It doesn't hurt that I've somewhat come to enjoy her company as well.

"Have you always been this...bold?"

"When you grow up in a family like mine, you have to learn to speak up and be yourself. Especially when you're surrounded by this group of men, they don't pay any mind to docile women."

"You could've fooled me. I thought that was what they hated about me. That Blaze and the others want me to be meek and opinion less."

"It's not that they want you meek or non-opinionated. They want the club kids to have a fair shot in school. They already put up with enough threats. They don't want to have to worry about teachers or whoever bothering them. Trust me, I was a club brat, I can attest that things were hard growing up. We were in danger plenty of times, not because of my father's love of motorcycles, but from enemies jealous of him, wanting to hurt him. School is one place we shouldn't have to worry about the kids having a rough go."

She continues, "You coming down on them and not backing down is what set you in the MC's sights. Had you just tucked tail, then none of the guys would've given you a second thought."

"I shouldn't have to, though. I have a right to stand up for myself and do what I believe is appropriate."

"Absolutely, and I agree with you unless it's a biased opinion. Which in this case, you poked the tail of a snake. You thought it'd slither off and leave you alone, but this snake has fangs—big fangs. You fighting back with the boys when they showed up, trying to offer the school support, got you bitten. Now that Blaze knows what kind of woman you are, he won't want to let you go so quickly. He wants to see how many bites you can take; he wants to know how strong you really are...if you're a worthy match."

"Match? You mean....? Wait, surely, you can't be serious."

"Oh, sweetie, I'm as serious as I can get. He sees you as a worthy opponent and an important thing about the men in this MC...they like conquering and claiming, then keeping."

"But I'm nothing like him," I attempt to argue. "I-I don't fit with his mold."

She shrugs, working at the tie on my wrist. "Then you should've thought of that before. You can't tease a tiger and not expect to be dinner."

"Why do you keep referencing animals?"

She meets my stare. "Because it's the best way to describe them. The men here are animalistic, they revert to their basic needs to protect, provide for, and claim. I have a suspicion that Blaze is in the provision stage with you. He's going to give you what you need, and he's already been protecting you from the club killing you. Who knows what he'll do when he gets home, but I have a decent idea."

"What should I do?"

"You can't do anything right now, but drink this delicious beverage I brought for you. I'm going to make you feel good. It won't seem so bad in a few minutes," she says, and I quickly agree, wanting whatever she has to offer. I'm not ready to think deeply into what Blaze's future plans are with me.

I take a sip, noting the flavor of alcohol mixed with the juice. It's early, but I'm grateful for it with the discussion we just had. I never drink this early in the morning, but I've also never been kidnapped in the past or outright cussed. I'll take whatever I can to get my mind off the revelations she just brought to light. This entire time I thought my attitude was putting Blaze off when, in reality, it was doing the complete opposite. I'm an idiot.

Blaze

We pull off a distance from a cluster of run-down apartment buildings. It seems pretty much abandoned, but I doubt that's the case at all. I'm sure these fuckers have eyes everywhere unless they're too stupid to believe they're untouchable. With the cartel, though, there's really no telling.

Exterminator taps his ear, telling us all to use the comm system he handed out when we parked. We're not supposed to spread too far away from each other, but it's better safe than sorry to have a good way to communicate with each other. Nightmare leads the way, strapped down like he's on a mission to shoot everything in sight. This is payback for him, even though the incident isn't related to his last trip down south. To him, every ride here is a chance to get a little bit of himself back.

I follow along, doing whatever they tell me to. I'm no one's bitch, but Ex heads up the Nomads, Ares is prez to his charter, and Nightmare is closer to both of them than I am. We have enough chiefs on this ride, I'll just stick behind them and do what they need me to. They'll be too focused on what's ahead. Someone has to watch our back, and I'm that guy.

Exterminator's gruff tone comes through my earpiece. "Heat signature's picking up five bodies inside. There should be more, but I'm not seeing them."

"I can scout ahead," Nightmare begins to say when I hear something coming from the left.

"Something's over here, nine o'clock," I reply, and Ares steps to my side.

"The fuck?" he mutters.

Ex growls, "Blaze, east; Ares, south; Night north." He orders, and I continue to stare in the direction of the noise. We collectively hold our breath, all peering in our specific directions. "Stay alert."

He doesn't need to say it; we're already strung so tightly we may pull a damn muscle.

"Meow" comes from the direction of the noise and sweat breaks across my brow. "Meow," is repeated, and we exhale with relief.

"Fucking cat," I mutter as the building beside us explodes and crumbles of debris rain everywhere.

"Fuck!" Ex curses as we fall to the ground. "Too fucking close, Spider! Chill out with the fuckin' drone," he hisses into his comm as gunfire rings out. "You were supposed to hit the other building, motherfucker."

I click off my safety, quickly glancing at my gun, and then prepare to shoot. It's been a while since I killed someone; the club's been drama-free for a bit. A scummy looking fucker comes running out using a whore as a shield. Without hesitation, I shoot through her, taking them both out. She may appear to be a shield, but you never know who's an enemy, and I'm not taking any chances.

"One," I count into the mic.

The other building explodes, making us all jolt.

Spider's voice comes through. "Five."

"Fucker," I retort.

"All right, ladies," Ares rumbles. "That leaves four."

"They're mine," Nightmare hisses. I roll my eyes. He's tripping if he thinks I'm not shooting what I see.

"You better shoot fast," I say, and he casts a deathly glower. I blow him a kiss, knowing it'll irritate him more.

Ex growls. "You're acting like some spoiled brats. Just shoot them so we can get the fuck out of here. And Spider, pay attention to the other groups. We've got this."

With a huff at his chastising, I scan my area. "I'm not seeing anything. You sure somebody else is here, and Spider didn't take them all out?"

"They're here, all right, hiding out like little bitches," he growls in return.

I'd be a little more convinced if I had a heat signature reader like he does. Exterminator chin-lifts to my right. I'm sick of the suspense, so I make my way, low crawling in the direction he noted. I come upon a half wall and quickly pop my head up, expecting to be shot at, but to my surprise, there's no rat-tat-tat of ammunition flying. This time I raise up a bit slower and peer around, looking for whatever he's picking up. I don't see shit.

Ex stares crazily and points off to my left a bit.

I glance that way, but there's still nothing. I shrug, casting him a look that tells him he's lost his fucking mind.

He returns my regard with an angry point directed toward the ground.

I haven't the slightest fucking clue what he means, so I hop over the wall completely, and as I land, there's a motherfucker waiting for me on the opposite side on the ground. It all happens so quickly. I don't have a chance to process much of anything; I just react. I think the dude's just as shocked to see me land beside him. He lunges, grabbing for me.

On reflex, I put my gun to the middle of his forehead and fire. Blood sprays all over the place, including my face. He collapses, lifeless, and no longer a silent threat.

Taking a breath, a smile overtakes my face that I didn't die. I quietly grumble into the comm. "Two."

Night's dejected voice comments, "Fuck you."

"You'll get one, *lil buddy,* don't worry," I reply sarcastically, knowing it'll chafe his ass.

I sit in place, catching my breath when gunshots ring out behind me. I don't want to chance my head getting blown off by looking over the wall, but I have to, in case my brothers need me.

Ares and Ex are crouched on the ground gawking at Nightmare. He's standing in the open, releasing bullet after bullet, looking more like some kind of angry Italian mobster in a shoot-out.

"The fuck's he shooting at?" I ask, flabbergasted, and they both reply with a confused shrug.

Ares mutters, "Ex nodded over that way, and Night went a little loose."

"Jesus," I murmur as a grimy cartel thug goes running. I guess he was the one hiding that Ex had been attempting to point out.

Nightmare roars and charges after him. He takes aim and fires, and the dude falls like a sack of potatoes. Night got him square in the back of the head.

Ares grumbles, "Sorriest bunch of cartel fuck faces I've ever seen." We easily agree.

Out of nowhere, two thugs rush Nightmare, catching him off guard and taking him to the ground. The big brute hits the floor, swinging.

"Should we assist or let 'em sort it out?" I ask, not sure if Night would beat our asses next for trying to help a brother out.

There's a shrilling cry of pain as Nightmare snaps one of the guy's bones like a toothpick. Ex shakes his head. "Nah, he's got it."

Spider comes over the earpiece. "I'm not seeing anyone else in the area. I think you guys cleared it, aside from whoever Nightmare is making squeal like a starving pig."

Ares gets to his feet. "Don't know if I should be offended or not, didn't even get a hit in." He sounds like a kid who lost out on the ice cream truck. While I'm over here, dirty and covered in someone else's blood.

Two shots garner our attention as Nightmare's back to standing and sinks the bullets in one of the guys on the ground. "We need this one to question?" he asks, not even winded from the scuffle.

Ex shakes his head. "Nah, we're just cleaning house at this cell. The few important guys should be at another location if they're here at all."

Night lets two more shots fly free into the sobbing mess of a man curled at his feet.

"Let's get the fuck outta here. I need a shower." I huff.

"Three," Nightmare retorts, and I send him a look that says, 'fuck off.'

"Agreed, let's ride," Exterminator confirms, and we make our way back to the bikes.

This job went exactly the way I like them to. I got a little dirty but didn't get a scratch on me. Now, I can finally get back to Amelia and figure out what the fuck to do with her. Thank God she hasn't the faintest clue of what a "job" entails; the bitch would fall out if she did.

"Brother." Viking gestures for me to enter his office. He's bruised up, took a bullet to the shoulder. Thankfully, that was all he brought back from our little road trip down south.

"'Sup, man?" I ask, chin-lifting to Princess. She's perched on his lap like a protective chihuahua. She about lost her shit, seeing Vike hurt. She's been glued to him since we arrived home.

"P took care of our principal problem while we were gone."

"That so?" My brow raises. I haven't even seen Amelia yet. We got back and had to patch the brothers up, along with drink a few beers. I know Princess would've looked out for Amelia, so I'm taking a bit of time to decompress before speaking with her. "Want to clue me in?"

He nods and gestures for me to come closer. He turns the open laptop around so I can see the screen. There's a video paused. I glance at them both. His expression's blank, but Princess's is serious. It looks like she's prepared for a fight, and I haven't the slightest idea why that'd be unless she hurt the woman in my room.

"The fuck is this?" I grow weary, worry clouding my mind over Amelia Stone.

"Hit play," he orders.

Releasing a sigh, I do as he's instructed. Female moans immediately fill the office, and I meet his stare again, confused. He nods to the computer, and I flick my gaze low, watching the screen. It's far out, the camera moving closer, slowly, so only sound comes through at first. I begin to notice something extremely familiar; it takes a second for it to register, though. As the images come into focus, it looks more and more like my room here in the clubhouse.

"Just relax and feel," Princess's voice comes over the video, then more breathy moans follow.

"Jesus," I mutter. "P?" I ask, wondering if it really is her that I'm hearing.

"Keep watching," she replies. I glance to my brother again, not wanting him to fucking shoot my ass if I see his ol' lady fucking someone. I've seen them together many times, but this shit is in my own room.

"It's all good," he grumbles, and my eyes move to the laptop again.

The video's a bit wobbly as whoever's behind it walks past my bed. There's the rope extending through the room I'd installed before I left and random shit thrown about. The moaning and shower spray gets louder as the person recording approaches my bathroom. They stop at the doorway, and then the video zooms in.

My mouth drops open.

Princess and Amelia are both naked in the shower, but she doesn't look like the stuck-up principal I've grown used to. This woman has her head thrown back, her face twisted with bliss. Princess fingers her while kissing over her breasts then moves lower. When she leans into the apex of her thighs, my eyes shoot to P's.

"The fuck?" I growl. "And why isn't she tied up? She could've escaped with all of us gone."

She shakes her head. "B had my back."

"Bethany was the one recording?"

Princess nods, and I glower at her ol' man. This shit is pretty fucked as I knew absolutely nothing about it. "I don't have to tell you to check your ol' lady," I begin, and Viking shakes his head.

"She had my permission," he admits, and my mouth falls open again, caught off guard.

"The fuck, Vike?"

He shrugs, wincing at the movement in his wounded shoulder. "Something had to be done with her; she's been here for a week already."

"It was motherfuckin' club business. We voted that I'd handle it."

Princess speaks up, although it's not her place when we're discussing club business. "Blaze, please just hear me out."

My brow's so high, it's got to be in my hairline at this point. I'm fucking pissed at her. I trusted her. If she were anyone else, I'd grab her and toss her outside on her ass, but Viking wouldn't stand for it. Besides, she's like a goddamn sister...I think that's why this bothers me so much in the first place.

She continues by saying, "You like her."

I start to argue, but she holds up her hand. I shoot a testy glance at Vike before meeting her eyes again.

"You do. You're being patient with her and coming to me for advice."

I glare. "Yeah, in fucking confidence!"

Viking interrupts. "Nothing's fucking confidential when it comes to my woman and my club."

I respond with a furious growl. My hands rake in my hair, clawing at my scalp. This is bullshit.

Princess's soft voice carries on. "You needed my help. You just didn't know how you needed it. I have a video now to hold as collateral. She can't mess with the Oath Keepers anymore, or we'll make it public, and she'll tank her career. You told me you didn't want to hurt her...well, now you won't have to."

"Bullshit! This will ruin her; I may as well slit her fucking throat."

Viking shrugs. "If that's what you think, but my Cinderella came up with a solution to our problems. I told her to do it so we could be done with this fucking woman. We have what we need, so now you can do what you want with the bitch. Fuck her, muzzle her, shoot her...I don't care. Problem solved in my book."

"And why do I need to do jack shit anymore? I had a job to do, or at least I thought so. I'm guessing you'll have all the ol' ladies take care of our shit now?"

He growls glaring. "Be careful what the fuck comes out your mouth next. And if they can take care of something that doesn't put them in any kind of danger, then fuckin' right, I'll let 'em handle it."

"Argh!" I explode, beyond furious. "Keep your woman out of my shit!" I yell.

"I didn't put her there. You did, motherfucker!" he roars back, and his words hit home. He's right, I'm the one who asked if I could seek her out. I never asked her to do this exactly, but I asked for her help. I never would've been okay with the video, and she should've talked it over with me...but Viking's right. That fact pisses me the fuck off, too.

I storm out, heading for the bar and as much whiskey as I can guzzle. I need to think, damn it. I can't believe this; I can still hear the moaning in my mind and see that shower image. It was hot as fuck. I don't know what I'm angrier over—the video or the fact that Princess was able to get Amelia to look like that, and I wasn't.

Blaze

The stool beside me moves, a big body filling the empty space. I'd know him anywhere; we've been around each other for far too long. He grunts, but I ignore it.

"What now?" he eventually mutters.

"You knew what Princess and Bethany were up to?" I ask, already aware of the answer.

He grunts again, in admission.

"You watch 'em?" The thought spikes a fiery bout of jealousy through my veins.

Torch shakes his head. "Nope. I stood outside your door in case the bitch made a run for it."

"You'd have killed her," I state, knowing him better than most.

He sighs. "Probably. Fuck, I don't know. Depends on if she'd have fought me."

I nod. "She would've. She's a feisty bitch."

He taps the bar top, gesturing for a drink. "I figure that's why she's got you so twisted up. Bitch is a nutcase."

Releasing a breath, my shoulders drop. "Fuck if I know, man. At this point, I don't have the faintest idea of what to do with her."

"Maybe it's time you fucked her."

"In the past, I'd have agreed with you, but now, I'm not so sure. Maybe she likes women" I rationalize, and he snorts.

"You two eye fucked each other from the first time you saw one another. Doubt she likes pussy that much." He shrugs, and I finally look over.

"You know, Torch, I think you may be right."

"I'm always right," he grumbles.

I ignore it and throw back the liquor that'd been placed in front of me. Princess has already got the leverage we need, so I don't have to worry about hurting Amelia anymore. I suppose that's true unless she gets brave and opens her mouth regardless of the video.

"You're too worried about what the fuck she thinks, I can see it all over you. Vike put you in charge to get this handled cause you don't give two fucks what anyone has to say. Now you've gone and let her weasel her way under your skin. You're upset about Princess, but I think you're damn lucky Bethany hasn't taken it into her own hands. That's her kid the principal's fuckin' with. I know damn well B wouldn't have gone with a sex tape; she'd have carved a chunk out of her."

I release a tense breath and agree with him. You know Bethany has to be crazy to be Nightmare's ol' lady. That dude is fucked in the head. I was close to him in Mexico when he went apeshit for revenge. Thank fuck we weren't storming a compound or anything; the fucker may not have made it back with his diva antics. Knowing Bethany, if we ever return without her ol' man, she'll poke holes in all of us.

"I swear these bitches around here are fuckin' nuts," I comment, and he murmurs his approval.

Could that be why she intrigues me so much? Her mouthy little ass with her nose stuck so far up in the air that it's amazing she doesn't have a kink in her neck...I find it sexy and a challenge. I want to bend her to fit me and to make her want me. I don't know why the fuck I care so much to make it happen, either.

"The ol' ladies took care of the shit work. You're not the bad guy anymore."

With a huff, I chuckle and argue. "I'll always be the bad guy in her eyes."

He tosses back his drink and meets my irritated stare. "Yeah, but do you fucking care? Stop giving a fuck and take what you want."

That gets me to shut up. He has a point. I don't give a flying fuck if she thinks I'm a bad guy; I am one, after all. I give a shit that she knows I won't hurt her, that I'm the one who can protect her and care for her.

Fuck...did I really just think of the words "care for her?" Jesus Christ.

"She even aware you're back yet?"

I shake my head.

He mutters, "Pussy."

"Fuck off. I never see you with a woman."

"You know Flame. Why the fuck would I want to chance getting tangled up with another psycho bitch? One in my life is all I'll ever need."

"She's locked up, brother."

"I know. I check that shit all the time just to make sure."

I can't help but laugh at his admission. Big, badass Torch got his ass handed to him by a petite firecracker of a woman. He's got her pegged though; the bitch really is psycho with a capital P. She ever got out and saw my brother with another chick, she'd light her up and watch her burn to death. I know that much from experience. Flame loves to set shit on fire.

Odin steps up beside me. "Brother." He puts his fist out.

Torch and I both fist bump him, and then we're interrupted by Cherry leaping at him. He pulls her in, wrapping his arms around her tightly, and suddenly, it's a little hard for me to breathe.

When in the hell did I start wanting that too? I'm a bachelor, and I've always loved living that life, but it doesn't seem to hold the same appeal to me any longer. Granted, I may not want to marry and have kids or anything right now, but I want to know I have someone waiting for me, who's excited to see me. I mean, Odin used to be just like me, not thinking twice about fucking whoever looks good that night. Now, he's busy spending his days building him and Cherry a house and shit. He's taking after Viking, looking to his blood brother for help in the relationship department.

Is it Amelia who's got me thinking this way? And why in the fuck do I have to desire the most difficult woman I've come across? This has to be payback for all the shit I've pulled in the past.

I grumble my goodbyes, though Odin couldn't give two fucks as Cherry's got his full attention. Torch, however, tells me to get laid and that he'll see me later. The man needs to take his own advice. I don't make it my business to know my brother's fuckin' habits, but his are obvious. We'd been debriefed as soon as we made it back, so I'm free to do whatever the hell I want. The ride home was long, and I was already exhausted from sleeping like shit and thinking about Amelia. Throw in the argument I just had with P, and I'm emotionally and physically beat.

I hit a guest shower, hoping Amelia's asleep and I won't wake her up when I head for my room. I don't want to talk to her right now. I've got too much riding on my mind along with residual anger from the goddamn sex tape. I was on the road and getting shot at while she was getting her pussy licked. That shit both turns me on and infuriates the fuck outta me. She's in my room, in my bed...by default, that makes her ass belong to me. I'm not generally a territorial person, but in her case, things have changed.

My room's dark and silent. I've lived here long enough to know my way around it. I'd forgotten about the rope, however, and run right smack into it. There's enough force, I know it must jostle her, yet the woman in my bed lies still as a statue. I bet the bitch is awake and pretending she's asleep. She doesn't want to greet me? That's just fuckin' fine. I'm tired and could use a full eight hours before dealing with her opinionated mouth. In this mood, I may end up shoving my dick in that hole if I don't sleep first.

I dump my bag off to the side of the door and yank the towel free from my hips. I toss it off somewhere into the darkness and walk until my knees hit my bed. I can make out the texture of the comforter, but everything else is pitch black. Most of our rooms don't have windows. It was supposed to be a safety precaution when the compound was built, but it also means our rooms have no light unless you flip a switch for it.

Crawling over the plush mattress, I practically dive under the fluffy down and rest my head on my pillow. It feels too damn good to be home, especially when there's a body waiting in my bed, and it's not a clingy club whore. Unlike them, Amelia doesn't beg me to put her on the back of my bike every time she's naked. On the contrary, the bitch is just egging to leave me. It's entertaining to have the opposite. Usually, I'm booting bitches out of my bed, but in this case, I've tied one to it.

I shake my head at the thought and close my eyes. I concentrate on her steady breaths, and before I realize it, the sound has lulled me into a deep sleep.

Amelia

The first thing I notice when I stir from sleep is the bulky heater next to me in the bed. *He's finally back.*

My body has a chill, so I turn into the warmth. Princess took my clothes away the evening before. It was the only clue I had that Blaze would be returning soon. I was sad to see the robe go, but a strange sense of excitement had begun to fill my stomach, knowing he could be back at any moment. What would he do if he knew I wasn't naked for the past few days? Would he punish me for not obeying him? The thought of him growing angry has my insides quickly heating up, and the juncture between my thighs tingles.

Orgasming each day has completely opened up my senses and feelings throughout my body. That and the thought of Blaze coming back has been at the forefront of my mind. It's hard to fathom that it's taken precedence over me getting out of here. At some point, I traded my desires from escaping to being near Blaze. When on earth did that happen, and why? I should absolutely despise the man lying next to me, yet I find myself curious about where he went and what he's been doing. Did he go off and see a woman?

If so, why does that thought irritate me so much? I should rejoice in him being with another lady, yet it makes me sick with envy. Maybe it's because he's yet to touch me, aside from having his hand lay over me when we sleep. The one time his fingers were on my pussy was when I deemed them to be there. I want him to reach over and finger my hole like Princess did in the shower. Maybe even put his tongue inside me too... I blame these intense feelings on him. I wasn't this way two or even three weeks ago; I was completely focused. Blaze has made me question nearly everything I know and have come to believe in. He's made me desire him, and that's the craziest part of all, me wanting some maniac biker as badly as I do.

I'm sure he'd laugh his butt off if he had any inkling whatsoever that he's turned the tables on me. It'd be like winning for him, I'm sure. He seems the type that's used to getting what he wants. After all, it drove him crazy that I didn't succumb to his charms when he showed up at the school with Annabelle Teague's father. *What kind of name is Torch, anyhow?*

His big paw jostles, moving to wrap over me. His fingers would be on my breast right now if I were turned over. The thought makes me want to move to feel him there, but I don't do it. I won't come off as desperate, although I sort of am at this point. I'm anxious for anything—his attention, his touch...just anything, as long as it comes from him. It shouldn't be like that; I'm not supposed to crave him. I know better. I'd be like all of those other women he's used and discarded after he'd finished using them, and I can't allow myself to be that. I'm stronger; I always have been.

I try not to move him much with my breathing. I don't know why I care if he has a decent night of sleep or not. Lying next to him while he looks so peaceful has me intrigued. The man is ridiculously good-looking when he's awake and spouting off about knowing what's best for me, but he's even more handsome when he's vulnerable and quiet like he is now. I can make out the small indentions where his smile and scowl lines normally are. I haven't witnessed him with a full-blown smile, but Princess has told me that Blaze is generally carefree around the clubhouse. I'd imagine if that's the truth, then he'd smile frequently.

She shared a lot with me while he was gone doing who knows what, more than she probably should have. Would he be angry if he knew that we were talking about him? I doubt he'd care, but part of me still wonders what he'd think about it. Was I on his mind the past couple of days as well? If he had another woman around then I doubt it, he seems like the type of guy who's used to having female company whenever he wants it. I don't know why that thought makes me so upset. It'd be completely out of line to bring it up, even though being kidnapped isn't exactly in line with any sort of rules I'd be familiar with. I think the most important thing to worry about in this situation is for me not to end up dead. Yet I find myself fuming over thoughts of him possibly being intimate with someone other than me.

His hand moves, flexing to bring me forward. He's a beast of a man, so his muscular arm easily scoots me closer to him. He could toss me around like a rag doll if he so desired. My breathing speeds up as his scent fills my nose, stronger than before. He always smells so clean and enticing, like bottled-up man. He grumbles in his sleep, leaning in to plant his nose to the top of my head. I should smell like his soap. Princess used it to wash my hair and body yesterday. Never mind that I was thinking of him while she did it. No one needs to know that fact aside from me.

We're so close now, I can feel him graze against different parts of my flesh. I'm feeling warm all over, maybe too warm at having him in my small bubble. I want to lift my leg and slide that hardness right inside. His cock has been large every time we lay together, yet he hasn't even attempted to use it. Why be naked like this otherwise? Is he using it to taunt me? It's beginning to hold merit; I want to rub my core on him like a cat in heat and then come all over the tip. This isn't right...he shouldn't make me have these feelings. I'm his victim, not his lover.

As if he can read my mind, his hand shifts down. His rough palm caresses over my silky-smooth skin, exploring. It stops at my waist for a beat and then lowers to cup my small behind. His fingers stretch to expand over the whole thing before sliding farther to fit in the crease of my thighs. His fingertips barely graze my sex as they move to hold my thigh. He pulls my leg to rest over his muscular thigh, the tip of his length reaching out to graze my clit.

That's it, though. He doesn't nudge me anymore, just lines me up exactly where I want to be and leaves me there hanging. Could he be dreaming? I tilt my hips forward just a bit to test the waters. I wish I could see his face to watch his expression. I want to know if he's about to wake up or not. I go off his breathing; it's deep and steady, comforting. I only need to rub him a few times, and I can come; I know it.

Flexing my pelvis, I move until my clit rests on the tip of his cock. Just the light graze of it has tingles firing through me. My opening clenches, wanting him to fill it. Wetness pools below; by the end of this, my thighs will be soaked.

I begin to shift my hips, moving in circles. The pressure on my clit, knowing it's coming from his cock, is intense. It takes everything in me to clench my teeth together and not cry out in my passionate, wanton state. He's just what my body needed first thing. The thoughts of him pinning me under him and thrusting inside my heat has lights exploding behind my eyelids. I've had my share of fantasies the past couple of days, and they seem to all stem around Blaze for some reason.

Shamelessly, I rub my clit against his shaft's head, reveling in the wetness that leaks from his tip. It's the perfect amount of lubrication to allow my nub to slip and slide around the bluntness. I get carried away with my movements, and his length slips below, prodding at my opening. A whimper escapes me as it takes everything in me to hold back from sliding down his girth. I've never had a cock so big in me before, and the thought has my chest moving against his with my increased breathing. My nipples scrape against the light spackle of hair on his torso. Everything about this man drives me crazy, each touch is lightning to my core.

What is he doing to me? I can't remember ever wanting someone this badly before.

I'm so close. I make myself slide back up his length and let my clit ride his head again. I can't afford another slip, or I won't be able to hold myself back from having all of him. The sensations against my nipples has me imagining his mouth sucking on them, his teeth biting down on each stiff peak, and I completely lose it.

I lean in until my nose grazes his hot flesh, and I inhale deeply. His scent, his cock dripping precum, and the thought of his mouth on my breasts has me rubbing all over his cock needing more. I want to open my mouth and sink my teeth into his flesh. I can picture how he'd taste, how he'd feel in my mouth. I salivate as everything else around me blanks out, and my orgasm fully takes over. His hips push forward once, long and hard and I'm able to finish coming against him. It's like his body knew I needed the extra pressure to finish.

I'm panting, my cheeks on fire as reality starts to seep back in. My nose was pushed up against him hard enough; it had to disturb him. Leaning back, I glance upward to see if he's still sleeping as deeply as when I started. His cobalt orbs meet my eyes, fully awake. There's a burning inferno reflected back. My lips part, moving to say something...but I'm at a loss for words.

What could I possibly say about what just happened?

Amelia

He doesn't give me the chance to dig myself further into my hole of mortification. He moves swiftly, diving down below, and in the next blink, his mouth is on my core. His tongue lashes like a man starved as he promptly licks my juices. His tender, full mouth sucks at my pussy lips, desperate to not leave a drop behind. The groan of ecstasy he emits when he laps at my heat shakes me all over, making me wish I'd gone ahead and sunk his thick cock into my pussy moments before.

In mere seconds, he's making me orgasm again. I've had two in a row, and the sensations are so good it has my head spinning. Is this why he wears that infuriating cocky smirk of his whenever he sees me at the school or he thinks he has a valid point? He knows he's just that good, he can make a woman come with the snap of his fingers?

"Blaze," I cry out, not sure what to say or do, and not wanting the intense sensations to fade. They do, of course, and I'm left breathless, wondering what will happen from here.

He sits back, resting his naked butt on his heels. His cock juts out like a beacon, promising my body everything it desires. Breathing heavily, his fierce stare rakes over me from top to bottom, pausing on my parted legs.

"Blaze?" I whisper.

He shakes his head. "I need a shower," he practically growls and jumps up quickly.

"What? Why? Where are you going?" I call, watching his gorgeous behind as he makes his way to the bathroom. "Blaze! Stop and speak to me!" It's the first real order I've given him since I've arrived, the rest were broken pleas and pride, but this is me demanding him to listen.

He spins around, face red, muscles flexed. "I need to shower *now.*"

"But don't you want me?" I question, afraid he'll say no now that I'm making myself vulnerable to him.

"Of course, I do, but I told you I wasn't going to have you until you asked me for it."

"I'm asking," I admit breathily. "I want you to touch me."

He shakes his head, being the stubborn male I've grown used to. "No, not yet."

My mouth falls open. "But...you just said...I told you I wanted you."

"Oh, no, babe, you told me you wanted it."

I nod, not understanding what the issue is. He's being difficult. "And?"

"And you'll have to fucking beg me before I put my cock inside your pussy. I told you, I don't take pussy, yours included. When you beg me, I'll know you're ready for it."

With a frustrated groan, I fall back against the pillows and roll my eyes. He's being ridiculous right now. I gave him my permission, yet he wants even more. "It won't happen, you know," I say loudly. "The begging. I won't do it."

With a disbelieving snort, he carries on to the shower, jumping in straight away. I hear him groan and then curse, "Fucking fuck, that's cold!"

"Wouldn't need a cold shower right now if you weren't so stubborn," I call out, and he replies with a disgruntled grumble.

He's stuck being frustrated while I just had two amazing orgasms. He obviously wants me; he's just making it hard on himself. At least I know now that he really won't touch me unless I want him to. Blaze is surprising, that's for certain, and I find myself growing fonder of the tenacious man. With that sated thought, I close my eyes and doze back off. I don't have to worry about him taking me against my will or anything—he won't even do it when I ask him to.

"You're annoying," I remark as Blaze enters the room with a couple of sandwiches and some chips piled high on two paper plates. He has a couple bottles of coke tucked under his arm as well.

His mouth pops open, surprised. "Me? You're off your rocker."

"Okay, I don't know what that means exactly, but I'm guessing it's not a compliment."

He sets the plates down on his dresser, shooting me a look with a raised brow. He hands me one of the bottles of soda and unscrews the cap on the other, taking a hefty gulp. He spins his finger beside his head, giving me the signal for "crazy."

"How can I be the crazy one? You're the one who has me tied up in your bedroom."

He shrugs. "I brought some food; I could've let you starve."

"Obviously," I bristle, and he shoots me an exasperated glower.

"You're getting mouthy," he points out.

I shake my head. "I've always been this way. I think you've forgotten that you don't intimidate me." I don't know where this newest bout of bravery has come from, but I'm going with it.

He snorts and hands me a plate. It's everything I'd never allow myself to eat before, but I don't exactly have menu options here.

"If I didn't intimidate you, then why have you been so freaked out?"

"There's a difference between being intimidated and fearing for your life and possibly being raped." My shoulders bounce with my explanation. "I know you aren't going to do either, so I don't have a reason to be upset. Well, aside from being kidnapped and kept away from living my life."

He shakes his head again, muttering to himself, "Fuckers were right about me goin' too easy on her ass." He's talking to himself, but it clearly has to do with me, and I need to know.

"Excuse me?"

He meets my gaze before grabbing his plate filled with three sandwiches and chips that are about to fall off everywhere. "Nothing you need to hear. Just thinking, maybe I shouldn't be so easy on ya. You need to be kept on your toes, or else you think too much."

"Easy?" I laugh, although nothing about this is funny. "I'm literally tied up twenty-four hours a day, for I'd guess over a week now. Someone else has to wash my body and hair, and I can't even unscrew the lid on a bottle." I tilt my head to the soda, and he bites his lip, attempting not to grin. It sparks my temper, and I huff, "I don't see what's so amusing about this situation. And thinking too much can be considered a compliment!"

His grin grows. I doubt I'll like whatever he's going to say next. "Sounds a lot like you're being pampered to me," he counters, and I balk.

"This is not my idea of a spa trip, pal!"

He chuckles, and I won't lie, I enjoy the sound. "Pal, hm? I thought I was the *heathen* biker."

I shrug. The movement's unlike me, but being around Princess and Blaze this past week has rubbed off on me a touch. "I wouldn't exactly rule it out, but I'll admit you've surprised me."

He grows serious, obviously not pleased with my comment. He should be, though. It's a good thing that he isn't as rough around the edges as I'd initially anticipated. "How so?"

"Well, aside from drugging me and tying me up, this hasn't been what I always pictured kidnapping would be. I assumed you'd rape me, beat me, maybe sexually defile me, and in the end, kill me. My remains and the case would be plastered across local news, and you'd be a fugitive."

His eyes grow wide. "I'm fucked up, but I'm not sick in my head. I can easily kill you without doing all that extra shit and not get caught in the process."

I point, though it doesn't hold the same value with my hands tied together and holding a coke. "See, exactly my point. And, aside from you being obdurate, you've opened my eyes to process things a bit differently. I still don't agree with you on everything, and I probably never will, but I understand a little better why you believe in the things you do."

"Ah, so I'm not some woman-bashing man, trying to hold all women back from evolving, you mean?"

I release a breath, wanting to point out a few things we still disagree on but refrain. Instead, I nod, and he rewards me with a real smile. The impact it has on me is intense too. It's like being hit with a sledgehammer, though I've never experienced that sensation, thankfully. In other words, it's beautiful and completely transforms his hard face into something a little bit breathtaking. I thought he was handsome in the past, but it had nothing on witnessing him like this. Happy...and if I dare admit, pleased with me. That feeling has warm tingles spreading all over me and my heart warming to him. My protective shell cracks a touch more, and suddenly I'm looking at him with hearts in my eyes.

How on earth did this happen? I want him, and not only for a quick morning orgasm. This is bad—really bad. I'm no longer hoping he chokes and dies on his next meal, but I'm wanting to make him something to see the appreciation reflected back at me. I'm wanting things that I was against when he first brought me here. At some point, I have to come to terms, is it wrong or behind the times if I want to do something for him? Is it truly bad if I want a strong alpha male to be next to me? Or in front of me to protect me, and at my back when I need him? He's pilfered away all of my arguments and made me doubt them.

"Eat, you need some meat on your bones," he comments, and I glance down. His observation has me questioning my appearance. I hadn't cared what he thought before, but now I do.

"You think I'm too thin?" I rebuke, on the fence of being offended.

His lips turn down as he takes a huge bite and chews. Once he's finished, he argues, "I didn't mean anything by it. I said it because you skipped breakfast. Weren't you ever told you'd have to keep rocks in your pockets from not eating enough or you'd blow away? You know...weird shit adults say to get kids to eat."

"So...you, uh, think I am attractive?" I glance at him through my lashes, both wanting and not wanting to know his answer.

"Fuck yeah, have you looked in the mirror?"

A smile breaks free, taking over my face like some lovesick schoolgirl with a middle school crush. His compliment shouldn't make me so ridiculously happy, yet it does. "You're not so bad either," I confess softly.

He huffs. "Not bad? Babe, you seen these abs?" He goes to lift his shirt, and I giggle.

Yep. I giggled. It's ridiculous that I can be deduced to act like this. I'm a strong, independent, career woman, who's goal minded and successful, yet here I am giggling over a man's sexist comment. I shake my head at myself. I'm morphing into everything I preached against. Funnily enough, I can't find it in myself to stop it from happening. This is my life right now; I'm going to go with it and worry about what happens tomorrow, tomorrow.

He flashes another smile my way, and I'm a goner. If he walked around wearing that smile all the time, I don't think I'd be able to speak much. He has this effect that makes me want to be quiet and smile back. It's utterly absurd.

"Blaze?"

"Yeah, babe?"

I swallow, building up my nerve. Eventually, I ask, "Would you untie me, please?"

He immediately becomes serious. "You're asking me to take the ties off you completely?"

I nod, chewing on the inside of my cheek. He gazes at me for a few beats. I meet his stare head-on, not about to retract my request when it's extremely important.

"You gonna attempt to take off on me? You realize I'll have to tie you back up, and you may get hurt if you try anything, right?"

I don't like him voicing that aloud, but I get it. I'm in the middle of a biker club, filled with people who don't like me. I'm not leaving here until they deem it so, whenever that may be. "I understand. I won't try to run."

"You promise? A man is his word."

"I'm not a man, though."

"But I still respect you in the same sense," he reveals, and my chest blooms at his acknowledgment of thinking of me as his equal.

"Then, yes, I promise you."

He releases a breath, sets his plate down, and makes his way back to me. "Don't make me hurt you," he whispers, peering into my eyes. "Please." His cobalt irises shine with a warning and something else I can't pick out.

He pulls a knife free from his jeans and cuts the rope in half. It falls to the floor, and my shoulders slump overjoyed that I can fully relax my arms once again. It's like a weight's been lifted off me.

"Thank you," I murmur and lean in to press a chaste kiss to his cheek.

His eyes widen, shocked at my move. I can be tender when the occasion warrants. I'm not an unfeeling robot. If anything, having him take away my pills has released an abundance of emotions and feelings.

"Now, are you any good at cards?" I ask, ready to use my newfound card skills I'd gained from the girls on him.

"Oh, babe, you have no idea."

"Good enough to place bets?"

His grin is feral as he nods. "You're about to find out."

Blaze

She beat me. Of all things, I'd never expect this neurotic principal to beat me in a couple games of Bullshit. Not only that, but we spent the day wasting time by playing cards, laughing, and actually getting along. Not only am I completely on edge when it comes to wanting to fuck her, but then throw in the fact that I like her personality when she chills the fuck out. Now I'm a bit of a goner, and I'm not sure what to do with that fact. Would she ever accept me?

She's kept good on her promise she made to me on not attempting to get away. I've had a prospect posted outside my door each time I've left the room. Not that I think she'd make it far, but better to be safe than sorry. She's not aware of the video just yet, and I have a feeling that if she were to get out of here, she'd be contacting the cops immediately. We can't have that; I don't want to be locked up, and the club would come down hard on me for that big of a fuck up.

I want to trust her, I do...but I don't, not just yet. She hasn't asked me to let her go home since I've been back from our run, and that has my head spinning as well. In the past, the captive women begged and pleaded nonstop to be let go. Jekyll always had them killed in the end, but I won't be hurting Amelia. I don't care what anyone says if I have to stick to her ass like rubber cement to protect her, I will. I don't know where the intense necessity to keep her safe has evolved from, but I'm going to roll with it. I'm too old to fight against my gut feeling. I've learned over the years to listen to my instincts. When it comes to her, they tell me not to lose her.

"You ready to take care of that bet?" she inquires, smiling widely the next morning while we're lying in bed. She's mighty proud of herself for kicking my ass, even though it was only a couple of card games.

"I'm not licking or eating anything disgusting," I grumble, miffed at her well-earned gloating.

She shakes her head, ready to burst with a laugh. She revels in me being disgruntled far too much. "It's nothing like that," Amelia promises, and I snort, not sure I fully believe her or not.

"All right, shoot."

"You have to spend the day naked with me."

My brows shoot up. Definitely the last thing I was expecting to come out of her mouth was for me to lose my clothes. I'm naked frequently, especially when I'm chilling in my room. I'm either fucking, showering, or sleeping, so no need for anything covering me up. Her request isn't anything that'll be putting me out. If anything, I get to see her on edge a bit. I don't admit as much to her, of course, let her think she's got me out of my comfort zone. To be honest, I prefer being naked. I throw on clothes around her, not wanting her to be too uncomfortable, but that can easily change.

"Naked?" I repeat. "You're sure about this?"

"Mmhmm and no cheating. You have to stay that way all day, even when you leave the room."

Ah, the kicker...she thinks she's being sneaky tossing in that last bit.

My lips tilt as I think about Viking's cursing I know he'll do when I walk into the kitchen naked to get Amelia and me some breakfast. They've all seen my junk plenty of times. He'll bitch about it while the ol' ladies will roll their eyes at me. The club whores will giggle and then make me a few offers...so, yeah, being naked won't be quite that bad for me.

"Fine," I exhale, acting as if I'm put out by her terms. "A bet's a bet."

She beams excited.

"You come up with the other wagers yet?" We made three bets, and of course, each of those times, she won. The games I won were when we didn't make a wager. Funny how that turned out. I swear she must've cheated somehow—no one as goody two shoes and uptight as she is can win three rounds of Bullshit that easily.

"Maybe..."

I lick my bottom lip, curious why she suddenly seems bashful. "Let me have it, babe," I rasp, enjoying her like this. She's so fuckin' sexy, but when she looks all sweet and innocent, it makes me want to corrupt her prim ass.

"I-I want to touch your stomach."

A wide smile blooms so fiercely my cheeks hurt. A chuckle rumbles my chest. "Oh, yeah? These?" I point down at my abs, and pink dots her cheeks. *Cute, so fucking cute.*

She follows my finger, her eyes trained on my stomach. She breathily replies, "Yes."

"I can handle that."

She reaches out, and I stop her hand before she makes contact.

"But not right now..."

Her nose scrunches, and I chuckle.

"If you touch me there, now...you'd be getting more than you're asking for."

"Maybe I want more," she taunts.

I pull away the blankets resting over my hips to show her my engorged cock. It's angry and needy, pissed at me for not taking care of my desires sooner. I could fuck a club whore and get a quick release, but they aren't holding the appeal lately that they used to. "Trust me, you don't want me like this. It'd be a hard, tense fuck. I'd probably hurt you, and that's not the image I want you to have of me."

She looks like she's ready to pout and pounce on my cock, so I quickly hop out of bed, dead set on doing the right thing with this chick. I refuse to confirm her initial opinions of me being some unhinged *heathen* who can't control himself. I meant it when I said the bitch would have to really want it. She needs to be ready to beg me to sink my cock in her pussy before I give in and fuck her like she desperately needs.

After me licking her delicious swollen pink pussy yesterday morning, I can't help but keep torturing myself thinking of her flavor. I want more and badly. I lost control yesterday when I woke up to discover her coming all over my cock. I was damn near ready to explode and had she rubbed my head anymore, I would've. Licking her pussy was the only way I could keep myself from thrusting my cock into her. Tasting her turned me on, but it also gave my dick a chance to have some space too. I'd run to the shower as soon as I'd had her juices on my tongue, then I'd beat my dick so hard, it's a miracle I don't have a friction burn today from it.

If my brothers only knew the lengths I've gone to with this female, they'd give me hell for months to come, and hell, maybe even longer. Speaking of admitting shit, I need to have a serious chat with Amelia about this damn sex tape. It really fucking sucks, too, since I feel like we're finally making some headway together, and she's learning how to relax. This new information is sure to stir the pot and get her hating me all over again, even though it's not my fault in the slightest. It wasn't my plan, and fuck knows how Princess dreamed it up.

I rub out my aching cock, amazed it's not limp from jerking it so hard yesterday. It takes the edge off, but I'm still aroused when I eventually bail from the shower and dry myself off. *Looks like everyone who sees me naked today will get an eyeful of stiff dick too. Awesome.*

I grab us some grub and manage to procrastinate until after Amelia's eaten and showered to speak to her about the video. I won't lie, I'm not looking forward to her flipping her shit on me. I should probably tie her ass up again in case she tries to come at me. The last thing I want is for her to get hurt by her own hand or by mine restraining her.

I sit beside her on the bed and open with, "We need to talk." I wince at how cliché that shit sounds. I was too much of a wanderer in the past to have any convos like that with women, and for her to be the first, it's sorta eye-opening. Not that I want to upset women or anything, but Amelia seems to be the one who's different for me somehow.

She swallows, gazing up at me curiously. She quietly replies, "Okay?"

"It's nothing bad," I say, trying to comfort her and end up sighing. I cringe. "Well, fuck...it sorta is."

Her gaze widens as she folds her hands in her lap. Her legs are pressed together, her perfect tits just chilling in the open. I wish I could touch her right now, make her feel good, so this news isn't as tough to take. *I should give her some clothes, but fuck me, she's so gorgeous to look at naked.*

"While I was gone, something happened. You and uh, P, hooked up?" I ask, pausing as I try to word this correctly and not sound the least bit jealous. I am, though. Fucking shit, I wish it were me in Princess's place.

She seems a bit shocked, probably at the fact that I know of what has transpired between them. I hadn't mentioned it before now, so she probably thought I had no idea. *Should I be upset that she hasn't mentioned it to me? No, I'm not her boyfriend. That was her business, even though she's in my room, in my bed. Yep, I'm irked, all right. Fuck my life.*

"Right," she admits, staring at me, waiting for my reaction. I don't give her anything though, I'm trying to be calm, so she stays that way as well.

"I'm just going to say it. I'm not good at sugarcoating shit."

She nods pensive.

"It was all recorded. The club has it on video with you in a very compromising position. If you go to the authorities, tell anyone about being here, or give our club brats a tough time from here on out, the video will be made public."

She takes it in for a moment before asking, "You're blackmailing me? Was yesterday recorded as well? Everything I do in here?"

My shoulders bounce, I guess she could call it that. Blackmail, a threat, intimidation tactics, fear, extortion...it's many things. Apparently, my club doesn't give two shits that I come off as the asshole schemer with it either. I get it, though. It's my job to take a little heat for the club, we all have to pull our weight and do our share. "Nothing else has been recorded, and it won't be in here. You have my word on it."

Calmly, she asks, "Was this your idea? Did you set it all up?"

She's being far too calm about this. I don't know what the fuck to do about it, either. Is she gonna explode or implode?

"It doesn't matter whose idea it was; I'm executing it."

"Okay," she says randomly, breaking the tense silence. She glances around the room, processing. She appears to have a million things firing through that intelligent mind of hers, and I wish she'd say it out loud. I want to fix things, but I haven't the faintest fucking clue how to.

"What do you mean, 'okay?'" I'm damn near having to peel my jaw off the floor from her lack of a reaction. She's being too easy on me; she should be throwing shit or something of the sort. This isn't uptight principal behavior or typical ol' lady behavior that I've witnessed in the past. When they get pissed, they chuck shit or try to shoot you. Is Amelia about to pull the same thing on me?

"Well," she says eventually and lies back, gazing up at me. She's so damn beautiful, even more so like this, right here, right now. "I don't think this was your idea," she states firmly. "I think you're following orders, just like you did with the kidnapping."

My brow furrows, my lips turned down into a frown as I process what she said. Someone's been talkin'. They had to be. "How the fuck do you know it wasn't my idea to take you?"

"Like you said, it doesn't matter. What does is that it's all happened already. I don't want that video made public, so the only answer I can give you about keeping this to myself is okay."

"But-but you, ah, should be furious...enraged, even, at this happening. I was expecting you to attack my ass over this latest wrench thrown in"

"How can I be angry when I let it happen? I could've told her to stop at any time, yet I didn't. I didn't want her to; I enjoyed it too much. I've been lonely, just floating through my life, and I hadn't realized that much until I came here. Having Princess and you to talk to every day and even touch me...well, it's opened my eyes to some things."

"Yeah?" I ask on bated breath.

She nods and clarifies. "I don't necessarily like women in a sexual way, but I won't deny that it didn't feel good. At the time, I needed it, it made me let go of my fear. Are you angry about it?"

I instantly start grumbling about why I shouldn't care, as she's not my woman.

She rolls her eyes, a definite clue she's been spending a lot of time around P. "I may not be yours, Blaze, but we seem to have this...*chemistry.*"

"You're admitting it?"

"I am," she offers with a sweet smile.

"You can touch me," I murmur, wanting to feel her hands on my flesh right now. I want to fucking kiss her perfect mouth and rub her all over. I want to pull her to me and wrap my arms around her.

"Hm?"

"The wager from earlier; you can touch me now."

Her irises light up. "Oh, yeah, one of the *many* bets that I won." Her smile blooms wider as she reaches out again. This time, I don't stop her but lean over her a bit, so she can rub from my abdomen up and over my pecs. My nipples grow stiff at her brush, and I clench my jaw to keep from moaning and telling her I want more. That I want *her.*

She runs her nails over my flesh after her pass with her fingertips, and I release a low, satisfied groan. The sensations she sends through my body has me nearly purring with pleasure. I lean in closer. She doesn't shy away, so I lightly nudge the tip of her nose with mine. I want to take her so badly my hands curl into fists, squeezing to garner some patience.

My hand unclenches and moves to cup the side of her face, my thumb caressing her delicate cheek. I move in, putting my mouth to hers. I begin soft, slow, with a chaste peck. She'd kissed my cheek yesterday, and the thought of kissing her has been on my mind since that very moment. Amelia perks up, applying a touch more pressure, letting me know that she wants it too.

The last mating of our mouths was when I'd kissed her to shut her up. It was more one-sided than anything, and I revel in her wanting to reciprocate this time.

I move to draw her bottom lip between mine, nibbling before I release the perfect flesh. She responds by squirming underneath me and raking her nails over my abs. Her mouth parts, and I dive in. My tongue twists with hers, the breeding of our mouths completely consuming my thoughts. Nothing else matters but here and now, her and me, like this.

The chemistry between us is unlike anything I've felt before. She challenges me verbally along with her kiss. I want to consume her, and if she'd let me, I would. She's far too comfortable with being in control and implementing the boundaries of her relationships, but with us, I'm not going to allow it. She won't shut me out; I won't give her a chance to.

My free hand braces beside her, keeping me from squishing her, but I want to feel every inch of her. I allow my form to lightly relax into her, our nakedness coming in full contact with one another. My cock grows stiffer than before, wanting to take this further, but I have to be patient with Amelia.

She responds in kind, spreading her legs open more so I can rub my length against her. We each respond with groans, our kiss evolving into something much more erotic. My hips twist, pushing against her flesh that's quickly turning slippery. She wants it just as badly as I do.

But...I swore she'd fuckin' beg me for it, and I'm a bastard who revels in knowing she wants it. With one last grind of my cock against her warm, soaked core, I pull away. Her lips are swollen and pink as she gazes at me with a dazed expression. Any man who takes one look at her will know her ass is owned. She's mine, there's no doubt in my mind about it, she just has to realize it as well.

"Blaze?" she sighs my name, curious why I ended things before they truly began.

I sit back, taking deep breaths to abstain myself from having my way with her right here and now.

"Yeah, babe?" My voice is unnaturally deep and gravely.

"You don't have to stop..."

"Mm, I do."

Her nose screws up, displeased. She's fucking adorable when she pouts. "I don't understand."

I shrug. "You don't have to. I need to take care of something real quick."

"Right now?"

"Yep."

She closes her eyes for a beat, just as frustrated as I am at this point. She could change this if she'd give in and beg me for it. I have to steal away that last little bit of strong will from her before I know she can truly be mine. She has to be willing to give it all to me because once I claim her, there's no going back.

A brother's commitment means more than the average Joe, and she has to be ready to be my property. I'm trying to be patient with the stubborn woman, but I'm wound the fuck up inside over her. Princess and everyone else is right—this woman obviously came into my life for a reason. It just took me a minute to figure out what that justification was.

I head to the kitchen and chug a shit ton of ice water, attempting to get my mind right and off fucking Amelia Stone. I've been beating my dick so much lately that I know it won't help right now. I may tug the motherfucker off if I try to relieve myself now.

Heading back to my room, I nod to Frost for standing guard and notice my door's cracked open. I gesture to it, and he mouths, "Princess."

I move to push it open, but he places a hand on my arm before I make contact. I meet his gaze again, not giving two fucks about being stark naked. He taps his ear, and as he's doing it, I hear P and Amelia's voices clear as day. Maybe I'll wait for a few, I need to find out what the fuck they could have to say to each other.

Amelia

"You betrayed me, my trust," I declare adamantly as Princess waltzes into Blaze's room. I wasn't mad at Blaze over the video because I know it was Princess and Bethany who were at the root of this plan, not him.

She shrugs. Wearing a sneer, she argues, "You stressed out my best friend. She and Night have been through enough in their lifetime, they don't need to deal with your shit."

"Their son broke the rules! I wasn't singling him out; I was doing my job."

"Which is understandable. *But* when you found out who Maverick's dad is, you did single him out. You moved to expel him!

Mav is the sweetest little boy I know. He's also my godson, and I'll do whatever I have to, to protect my family."

"Look, I'll admit I was biased, okay? I understand now that it was wrong on my part to be that way, but that boy can't go around kissing sweet adolescent girls. It's a basis for sexual harassment, they could be bothered by it for the rest of their lives!"

"He's a little boy, for fuck's sake! Where the hell do you get off on taking the love out of a young child?" She fumes, growing angrier by the second. "You're upset because your trust was betrayed? *Bitch*, do you know who the fuck *I* am? You're lucky I didn't have one of the brothers slit your throat for going after my family! I wouldn't even have to get my fingers dirty to deal with you, but I went soft on ya. I fucked you and made a video of it to keep your ass in line. Blaze cares for you a considerable amount, too much to hurt you, so I stepped in and took care of it. You can hate me all you want, but trust me when I say it could've been *so much worse* than what you got."

I nod, not sure what to say. I'm generally not a confrontational person. I like to nip it in the bud before it gets to that point, but obviously, Princess is the opposite. I don't doubt it for a second that their revenge toward me could've been graver. I'm more hurt that I was obtuse enough to believe she was a friend to me in the first place, that I was making way here with anyone.

"And for the record, you're fortunate you had to deal with Nightmare on this whole situation. If Bethany had been off of work to take those calls from your office, she'd have shown up to those parent meetings and rearranged your face. And the kicker? You'd have not been able to do shit to stop her because in case you missed the memo, the Oath Keepers own the sheriff's department. Hell, the sheriff himself used to ride with my father back in the day, so, please, fuck with us some more."

"Why do you people resort to physical violence and these types of threats?"

She snorts. "Because some people need an ass-kicking to understand a point. You have your nose so far in the air, you need to be taken down a few pegs. Welcome to reality, where you're not the smartest person in the room. Where *your* actions have *consequences*. We support our community one hundred percent, but you painted us as the bad guys when we could've been your greatest asset."

"So, you became the bad guys since I saw you in that perspective?" I query.

She nods concurring. "We did. You wanted us to be a problem, so we became one. We were more than willing to help out the school as far as donating money, baked goods, food for the poor kids during the holidays, and even security, but you practically spit on us."

I shake my head. "I won't take bribes; it's against my morals."

"It wasn't a bribe...it was to show you that we care too, just like any other parent out there. We love motorcycles, we enjoy having fun and don't always make the best decisions, but we love our kids just as much as anybody else. Hell, probably more; family is absolutely everything to us whether you're our blood or our chosen family."

"I can see that now." I bite my lip, feeling true remorse for the way I've treated them before I actually knew the type of people they were. I judged them when it wasn't my place. "I apologize for any stress I've caused the parents and kids here. I should've at least given Blaze the courtesy of hearing him out."

"Thank you," Princess breathes out, letting her guard down a touch. "It'd go much further if you said that to Bethany, Nightmare, Torch, and Viking. This wouldn't be happening right now if you'd have given us a chance."

Tears crest as I lower my gaze to the floor and nod again. I can't believe how idiotic I've been. She's right about one thing; I thought I was better than them, and here they're still offering to help my school. Not only my school but the children who truly need it, and I was stopping that from happening with my stubbornness.

Blaze has proved me wrong in my skewed beliefs of the Oath Keepers, however. Sure, he's kept me locked away, but he's also shown me compassion the entire time I've been here. I can only imagine how horrifying it could've been if someone else had gotten angry and kidnapped me. I could be dead, raped, mutilated, frozen, or who knows what, right now. Rather, I've got a full stomach, a comfy, clean bed, and people checking on me to make sure I'm okay. It's a bit ironic, actually. I can't remember the last time I had nothing to worry about, and being here has started to take most of my stress away, especially now that things are evolving with Blaze. I was under duress in the beginning, but it was all manufactured in my mind—I was never in any real danger so long as I did what they asked of me.

"You said he cares about me?" I question, wondering how true that really is. Ever since she said it, it's stuck with me.

She nods. "He used to not think twice about hurting women, but he's changed. With you, though...he'd take a bullet for you. I know it." Her brows raise as her hands rest on her hips. "And I'll tell you right now, you better fall in line if you plan on sticking around. It doesn't matter how much Blaze loves you, I'm the Ice Queen around here, and I can make your life a living hell. That man deserves something special, and so help me, you better be that *special*."

I swallow, my throat is tight and dry. She said he *loves* me. I can't help but feel warm with that notion. Could she be right about Blaze's feelings? And if so, what does that mean exactly?

I'm used to running the show, but clearly, around here, it's Princess's rule when it comes to the women of the MC. I have to admit, I respect her. She's stepped in and taken care of things for her family and their club. It takes a strong, intelligent woman to do that. Even *I* can see that much. "I may not like that you made the video, but I recognize why you did it. It still hurts since I allowed myself to be vulnerable with you, but I respect you for taking care of your family."

She nods. "I will always do what I need to for them."

"Then, they're lucky to have you."

Her hands release her hips, falling to her sides. She's let go of some of the tension and anger she'd been wearing when she'd entered.

"You truly believe he loves me?" I probe, and the door opens.

Blaze comes in. "P?"

She sends him a radiating smile, and if she weren't already married, I'd be twisting with jealousy. "Just checking on your captive." She sends him a wink. He smirks in return. "Wow, you're, uh...naked too?" She chuckles, shaking her head at him.

He nods. "Yeah, turns out Amelia knows how to play a game of Bullshit."

Her brows hike again. "Mm, you don't say?" She glances at me, surprise coating her gaze. She and the other ol' ladies are the ones who taught me how to play. "And you lost?" She teases him.

"Did *Teach* make a bet with you as well?" Teach is the nickname the ladies gave me when we were playing our card games. I tried to explain I'm a principal, but none of them were hearing it.

He nods, his cheeks tinting pink. He's cute like that, versus his usual sexy, smirking self.

"Well," she grins, flashing a glance at me, "looks like there's hope for you yet." She meets Blaze's gaze again, saying, "I'll leave you to it. My ol' man will castrate you if he discovers that I'm in your room with you naked."

Blaze grunts. "Yeah, uh, please leave before that happens." He chuckles and gestures to the hall.

She sends me a quick, serious look before striding through the doorway, calling out a cheery, "Have fun," in her wake.

My eyes find his, and I can't help but wonder if she's right. Does he love me? And if so, do I love him too?

"What's happening today?"

"Why do you think that today's any different than yesterday?" Blaze asks.

We've fallen into this routine, being trapped in his tiny space together. I wake up warm and completely turned on in his arms. Today was no different. I couldn't resist rubbing his length against me until he'd spilled himself over my thighs. I don't remember ever desiring a man as much as I do Blaze. Yet, he's stubborn and holds out from penetrating me. I don't understand it; he should be well aware by now that I want to have sex with him.

My lips tilt into a slight smile, and I find myself peering up at him through my lashes. When did I become that woman? Biting my bottom lip, I shrug, clasping my hands behind my back. I'm on full display for him, but it's not an issue anymore. I've been naked in front of him for far too long to over analyze what he may think about my body. He said he likes it, and considering he's hard around me daily, I believe him.

His cobalt irises flash to my chest, his Adam's apple bobbing as he takes my breasts in. He loves them. We've had some pretty heavy make-out sessions the past few days, and he's always licking between my thighs and sucking my nipples.

"I think your time here's almost come to an end." His cerulean orbs meet mine, serious. It was the last thing I was expecting him to say. In fact, I'd begun to wonder if he'd ever let me leave. I've grown used to being around him all the time, I don't know what it'll be like to go back to before. I'm not that same person anymore. Of course, I don't let him know any of those thoughts and feelings. I do want to be able to leave his room at some point in my life, even if I've grown comfortable around him.

"Is that so? Have I passed all of your requirements?"

He licks his bottom lip, fire back in his stare. "Not all of them."

"Oh? What exactly haven't I done that you wanted?"

He shakes his head, resting his hands on his hips. I push my chest out a bit more. I want him to keep looking at me like that. It makes me feel desired and sexy.

"I haven't felt that sweet pussy of yours wrapped around my cock yet."

My smile grows. "I can recall a multitude of times that I've told you I want more, to go further."

"Mm," he grunts. His hand moves, reaching out to touch my core. "You wet right now?" he rasps, and I pant, my vision going hazy as his fingertip teases my clit. The digit slides lower, through my lips to feel my entrance. He groans. "Fuck, babe, you are."

My palms move to his pecs, they're muscular and his nipples are pierced. It turns me on like crazy. He's everything I'm not—the yin to my yang. Leaning in, I press up on my tippy-toes to brush my mouth to his. Pausing against his lips, I whisper, "Please?" I've asked for him to go further, but each time he holds back, telling me it's not enough. It's to the point that when he puts his hands or mouth on me, I feel like my body and my core is going to combust.

His nostrils flare, his irises blazing. "More," he growls, the order making my body shiver and my nipples pebble. He's always quick to order me around. It used to infuriate me, but now it drives me crazy in an entirely different way.

"Please?" I whimper, ready to beg at this point. I need to feel him everywhere. It's like the thought has begun to consume me.

"Fuck," he gasps. "I love hearing you say it like that. You want me to fuck you, babe?"

"Yes, badly," I admit, crossing everything I have in hopes he'll finally surrender and offer up what I so desperately crave.

"Then say it again," he rumbles, and my brows jump.

"What?"

He pulls his mouth back a touch, and I panic, not wanting him to stop and leave me hanging again. He's done it so many times that I've felt like pulling my hair out. Scrambling, I plead with the first thing that comes to mind. "Please? Please, Blaze? I-I want you; I want you inside me."

His grin is feral as his hands wrap around me, locking tight. He grabs me into his arms, and then we're moving. He's ambling toward the bed, hauling me along in his muscular hold. My naked form presses against his sturdy frame, and I want to rub all over him. He's in a pair of jeans and nothing more, the faded denim material hanging dangerously low to show off his V and chiseled abs.

He tosses me to the bed; I bounce, and my mouth falls open with surprise. I wasn't expecting him to just throw me on here. Then he's climbing over my body, wearing a cocky smirk that I find increasingly tempting the more he does it.

He comes at me, expression fierce. He's on a mission, I don't know whether to be more turned on or scared at how intense he is. He takes my mouth in a blistering kiss, his tongue practically lashing at mine. It's all consuming. I can't think of anything beyond him, here in this very moment. My heart thunders in my chest, my hands shooting to his shoulders. I have to hold onto something, as he's moving full speed ahead. This is a new level compared to everything we've done already. He's on a mission. It's beyond hot to witness him just as turned on as he makes me.

His mouth takes a path lower, sucking and nipping along my throat. "Oh!" I cry out, loving the impression he elicits through my body. "I-is this really happening? Finally?" I manage to pant out loud with a breathy stutter.

"Mmhmm. Told ya, babe, you had to beg. Once you whimpered that sweet little *please*, I was ready to sink my cock in your pussy."

"Please." I do it again, now aware of how much it affects him.

He rumbles with a pleased growl, and his finger breaches my entrance. It's the first time he's ever fully penetrated my core. Before, with his tongue, he'd only play with my clit and suck on my lips to clean my juices. Stars fill my vision at his long, thick finger pushing in as deeply as he can.

"Oh! Yes! B-Blaze, please don't stop!" I plead, wanting anything and everything he'll give me at this moment.

"I'm not stopping, Amelia; I've just begun with you." He continues to move his fingers inside me until I'm spasming around him with my first orgasm. It's quick and intense, but that's how they all seem to be when it comes to him touching me. The man is magic in the sex department.

He allows me to ride out my orgasm before pulling away to lick his fingers clean and flick the button free on his jeans. He doesn't bother to unzip them, he just shoves the pants off his hips. His muscular thighs come into view as he works to push them all the way down. He kicks his jeans free, and they fly off somewhere into the background.

"Wow," I whisper as I rub my hands over his form. I've felt him before, but like this, it's just different somehow. Maybe because I know we're finally taking this all the way.

His cock head plays at my entrance, the tip slipping just inside my hole from my wetness. His hips shift, but he doesn't slide in any farther. My chest rises and falls with the intensity. I can't believe he hasn't just rammed right inside. Surprisingly, I want him to.

Blaze groans, clenching his eyes closed for a beat and exhales heavily. "Goddamn," he mutters under his breath before he shifts again. His arm flexes above me as he uses one hand to grab onto the headboard and the other to grasp my hip. He's remarkable. I've never seen so many muscles on display in my life. You'd think the man is carved from stone with how absolutely perfect every inch of him is.

The headboard creaks, and my eyes jump to the spot his hand grips onto. "Did the bed just break?" There's no way that sound was from the wood flexing under his hold alone, there can't be. I know he's strong, but...breaking the headboard?

He shrugs, his eyes glittering with desire. "Not worried about it, babe. You sure you're not a virgin?" His hand strays from my hip to grip his girth. He's big in all places, did I mention that before? He works to fit inside me, and a blush steals over my body. I didn't think I was this tight; the men in the past never had to put forth much effort to fit inside me, but they weren't this size either. Normally, I'd just tell them what I wanted, have them lay on their backs, and then take what I needed. With Blaze, however, I doubt that'll fly. He likes being in control far too much.

"I'm not a virgin, you're just bigger than the men in the past," I admit, and it strikes a wide, pleased smile from him.

"It's those frail beta-bitches, babe. You're not used to real men. It's all good, I'm happy to be your first." He winks and continues, "I'm only seven and a half inches long, but I'm as wide as a monster."

"A monster sounds about right." I try to lighten the tone and huff out a laugh. I won't lie; it stings a bit with each inch he pushes inside me.

"It's as wide as a canned Coke, babe." He chuckles and flexes his hips. The move pushes him in fully, and I cry out, my muscles tightening up. The feeling is unreal, he's right; I've never had anything like this before. The fullness of him has me ridiculously turned on and my core spasming. He doesn't have to do anything, just stick his cock inside, and I'm already coming.

"Oh, my!" I call loudly and bite down on my bottom lip. I may tear it in half at this rate.

"Fuck, you're squeezing me so tightly, you feel fucking great." He moves, pulling out a bit and then thrusting forward. It sends me spiraling, and in the next beat, I'm screaming, clawing at him as bliss hits me harder than the time before. My head flies back, but I fight it, not wanting to take my eyes off his physique.

"Please, please, don't stop," I plead. I'd never thought I'd so willingly beg and from a man to boot. He's making me come twice in a matter of minutes; he wasn't exaggerating about knowing what to do with women. I don't want to think of him with anyone else right now. Here in this moment, he's with me, and that's all I care about. Besides, when did I become territorial with Blaze, anyhow?

"Don't you worry; I won't be stopping anytime soon," he repeats, and I sigh, content with him having his way with me.

He plunges ahead, and the bed shakes, the headboard slams into the wall behind. It makes a thundering clap, my eyes widening with it. He just shrugs, offering me a cute smile and fucks me into oblivion. He wasn't fibbing about not stopping, and, well, I won't be walking straight anytime soon because of it.

Oh, and I was right, he broke the headboard.

Blaze

Church...

"What's the deal with the Cartel?" Nightmare asks Viking. Everyone's attention trains on the Prez to hear what he has to say.

He chugs some of his bottled water, briefly glancing around the table before gruffly answering. "We accomplished what we set out to do. We threw a wrench in their plans that they didn't know was coming. That being said, we've learned that the fight with the cartel is never-ending."

"What're we going to do about that?" Odin speaks up.

"We're going to do what we needed to do years ago. We're going to keep fighting to protect what means the most to us—our family and club. We're going to assist whoever we can in cutting the head off that southern snake. We caught a piece of its tail years back when we hit that heroin compound, and shit was crazy...this last job, we took chunks off its body. We need to keep chipping away until we get to the end and figure out a way to take out the cartel's leaders. Then it'll be maintenance work to make sure they don't regroup to remain intact with another leader. Where one falls, another takes their place."

Mercenary grumbles. "Since when is it our job to take care of this shit? We don't get paid to do the government's work."

Vike's brows jump, his glare pinning on the newer member. "We recovered three hundred sixty-two thousand dollars on this run. The boys and I found it at our cell we were hitting. According to Exterminator, what we find, we can keep. It'll be split between the Nomads and both our charters."

"Holy fuck," Merc responds, and the prez nods.

Viking continues. "We aren't being paid, but if we happen to step on a few million or anything else of value, we *can* be paid. Each run will be put to a vote, just remember that when we aren't on our guard, our clubs can get hit with blowback. When we aren't finding cartel dough to fill our wallets with, we're running guns, moonshine, and whatever else we find, and chancing prison time. Both are dangerous, both have risks...it's up to us to decide what the fuck we want to do to make our money."

Smokey coughs out, "We're looking at a sixteen-thousand-dollar payout from this run alone. That's taking some cash away for the various families and other interests the club has previously voted to support. Each active member will get an individual sixteen-thousand-dollar chunk of cash, give or take a few."

My mouth pops open; that's a damn good surprise bonus.

Viking grunts his agreement, and the brothers' moods seem to lift immediately.

The Nomads standing and sitting wherever they'll fit, fist bump each other. They're just as pleased with the news. The more cash they have, the more they get to ride off into the sunset and do whatever the fuck they want to.

The prez nods to Exterminator. He shifts, uncrossing his arms from his chest, and says, "We'll take a little time off and recoup. I'll keep up with my contact, and as soon as I know more, Vike will be made aware. The Nomads won't be leaving the charters high and dry, we'll be back up as much as you need us. You're all taking a chance on helping us out down south, and we'll repay in-kind. A frequent route for us moving guns is I-10, and if the cops are happy down there, then they stay off our backs."

Viking gestures at the burly man again then moves on. "Next set of business is this school bitch." His gaze trains on me. "You figure that out?" He knows as well as I do that his ol' lady took care of the issue. I guess he's not going to embarrass me in front of the brothers, though, and make it known.

I nod. "She won't be bothering anyone at school or elsewhere. You have my word."

Torch chin-lifts in my direction and mutters, "Thanks, brother. Annabelle will be able to relax finally."

I shrug it off and turn to Viking again. "I have something to say about her, though."

His brow wrinkles, waiting.

"She's mine," I declare coolly. I flash a glance at Torch and Nightmare to see their reactions. They're both stunned as they gaze at me like I've lost my head.

"Yours?" Viking rumbles. "As in?"

I nod. "I'm staking claim."

He snorts, and Nightmare barks out, "That prissy bitch will never let you touch her in front of anyone."

Torch mutters, "She'll probably ask you to book an appointment or fill out a record sheet, then call the cops on your faded ass."

"I'm not faded, dick," I growl in return. "I want her, so I'm keeping her."

"That so?" Viking asks. "You planning on letting her leave your room, or is this relationship going to be extra fucking twisted?"

My glare lands on him next. "I'll let her leave. She knows the deal, and if she fucks up, I'll remind her."

He shakes his head, glancing at the ceiling, then sighs. "You know what? I don't even fuckin' care. You want her? Fine, fuck it. *But* if she fucks up and gets this club in some shit, you have to be the one to put her six feet under. You feel me?"

I concede. I already know it'll never come to that. "I'll handle her. She needed someone strong in her life to get her to calm the fuck down. Trust me, she's chilled the fuck out. Still feisty and strong-willed, but she knows to lock that shit down where the club is concerned."

He grunts, "Good."

Saint grins. "I wanna see you fuck her, especially with the stories we've heard. You sure that bitch won't be the one on top?" He mocks, and I roll my eyes, giving him the finger.

"Fuck off. She knows who the man is."

Nightmare huffs, clearly not convinced.

"It may take a little while...but it'll happen," I defend.

"All right, then, fuck," Viking mumbles and asks, "Anything else?"

No one speaks up, so he gestures to Odin that he's calling an end. The gavel slams down, and he does his usual gruff bark of, "Get the fuck out!"

We pile out into the bar, and I can't help but be a tad miffed at the brothers, not believing in my charm where Amelia's concerned. They don't know what's transpired between us these past few weeks. I had her call in today and request another week of time off. She even lied to say she had a family emergency. There wasn't one; she's just not ready to leave our little world. I may've told her to do it and stood beside her to hear what she'd said, but she still did it. She could've told them anything in the span of the few minutes, but she told them exactly what she was supposed to.

She's no longer my captive, even though she wants to pretend that she is. In reality, she could throw on some of my clothes and walk right out the main entrance, and I wouldn't stop her. We have the video of her, and I know damn well she won't allow it to jeopardize everything she's worked for. She'll keep it quiet and do as she's supposed to, to avoid the repercussions.

I think it's time to take it to another level between us. I've slept beside her for two weeks straight. I've fed her and fucked her delirious. Now, she needs to be put on the back of my bike. She needs to feel the vibration between her thighs and the wind in her hair. Afterward, she needs to be thoroughly fucked, so she realizes that it's not something insignificant, that she truly does belong to me. I'm far too invested at this point; I don't think I could allow her to leave me for good if she were to make an effort to. My twisted heart just won't allow it. I want to keep her.

I will keep her...forever.

"That was intense!" Amelia exclaims, breathless and beaming a smile. We just got back to the club after our first ride together. She was glued to me, her body fit to mine like a glove. It was as if she'd meant to be there all along, and my chest had never felt so full having her arms wrapped around my waist as she'd clung to me.

"Yeah? You liked it?"

She squeezes my arm excitedly, irises glittering from her adrenaline. "I truly enjoyed it. I can understand why you all are so passionate about it."

"Something you can see yourself doing on the regular?" I try not to get my hopes up too high, but I need to know if it's a possibility.

"Oh, definitely. In fact, perhaps I'll look at getting one of those scooter types."

I immediately groan, my hand moving to my forehead. "Fuckin' shit, woman, don't do that."

Her gaze flashes to me again, full of confusion. "Do they not do the same thing, only at a safer speed? I could get a matching helmet and a jacket. Maybe even fake leather if it's a sensible color."

"Christ...not just no, but hell nah. I'll get you a good jacket, you don't want fake shit cause it won't hold up. As for the scooter, let's just pretend that you didn't say that. Damn sure don't say anything of the sort in front of the brothers."

"But I want to be animal friendly. I could just get some padding or something, right?"

I shake my head. "Babe, let me handle the biker shit, 'kay? I'll hook you up with what you need. As for the bike, you'll ride with me."

"But I was thinking of driving it to and from work..."

My brow wrinkles. "Like I said, you'll ride with me."

"What if I need to pick up my lunch?"

"Call me. I'll make sure you're fed."

She huffs out a quiet laugh. "You plan to wait on me outside of this place as well?"

I shrug, 'cause I'd been thinking of it. "Babe, it's my job to take care of you."

She starts to open her mouth to argue, and I hold up my hand to quiet her.

"Not 'cause you can't handle it yourself, but because I want to. I'm a fucking man, let me be a man for you. We already discussed this over and over."

She stares at me a moment before finally nodding. "Does this mean you're letting me go home soon?"

I shrug again, not wanting to admit that she can leave. I have enough on her that she won't fuck with the Oath Keepers in the future, but I don't want her to leave. It's strange to admit, but I'll actually miss her. I've grown so used to seeing her each time I enter my room, that it'll feel lonely without her presence and mouthy stubbornness.

"Oh, Blaze!" she exclaims and wraps her arms around me. The hug surprises me for a beat before I turn and pull her into my embrace.

"Hm?"

"You've been different today."

"How so?"

"Well, for starters, you gave me some clothes and took me out of your room. You let me ride on your motorcycle, and now you implied I may be able to leave soon. I miss my job and my bed."

"Mine isn't so bad, is it?"

She offers a tender smile. "No, it's not."

"I can sense a but in there." I drop my arms and commence walking toward the main entrance of the clubhouse.

"Blaze, wait." She reaches for me, her hand landing on my bicep, and I pause. She steps beside me again, reaching for my face. She turns my chin until I meet her gaze. "I still want to see you."

My brows raise.

"You've become someone important to me."

"Hm?" I grunt.

She grins. "I know, but it's true. I care about you. We may be opposites, but I feel something *here*." She places her free palm over her heart, and my protective wall completely crumbles where she's concerned.

I turn to her, my hand carefully cupping her cheek. Leaning in, I whisper against her lips, "I feel it there too." And then I'm kissing her like she's my everything and she always will be. I don't know when it happened, but at some point, things evolved, and I fell for the strong-willed woman. Pulling away, I admit softly, "There's only one way I can keep you."

"Anything..." she declares adamantly, and I chuckle darkly.

"I have to claim you...make you my ol' lady."

Her nose screws up. "Marriage?"

I scowl. "Hell no."

"Oh." She seemed opposed, but I can see her expression falter a bit. She wanted to hate the idea, yet she didn't, not deep down.

"It's more than that. Me claiming you means more than me putting a ring on your finger. You become my ol' lady that makes you family to the entire club. There's no turning back, we're together for life."

"Wow," she sighs, and I nod. "That-that's intense. And I'd be yours forever. You wouldn't get bored and cheat on me or anything? It seems like a lot for a man to commit to."

I scoff, wearing a disgruntled scowl. "That's why we don't claim a woman until we're sure she's everything we can't live without. Fuck no, I wouldn't cheat...some do, sure, but that's not me."

Her bottom lip wobbles, her gaze turning dreamy. "You think I'm everything you can't live without?"

That's what she heard? Not the rest? I shrug, reaching out to squeeze her hip. She's in my oversized T-shirt and a borrowed pair of leggings from Jude. "I mean...I wouldn't think about claiming you if I didn't feel that way."

A tear falls, cascading over her perfect flesh and then her mouth is on mine again, and she's kissing me with so much fervor my cock grows rock hard. My jeans squeeze the fuck out of it. I move to scoop her up into my arms. I kiss her fiercely, walking to the clubhouse at the same time. I'm done fucking around.

Flinging the door open, not breaking our kiss, the heavy door bangs closed behind us. Amelia jumps in my grip, but I hold her to me, not letting her break away.

"Nu-uh," I murmur, taking her lips, tugging them between mine to suck and nibble. My hands rake up her back until I get to the collar. I grab it with both hands and rip the fuck out of it. She moans at my savagery, rubbing her cunt against my abs. Shredding the material away until her back's exposed, I walk to the closest table and lay her down. She stares up at me, eyes dilated and chest heaving. She's so goddamn turned on, it makes me horny as fuck.

When I take her in, I immediately think that she's absolutely magnificent. She's different from anyone else I know, and it's intriguing. She never bores me; she keeps me on my toes constantly. "So fuckin' beautiful, babe," I murmur.

She bites her lip, smirking, looking like a motherfucking vixen ready to consume her prey. I'm so enraptured with her I don't realize the bar's gone completely silent to watch us. There're brothers and ol' ladies all over the place, but I couldn't give two fucks about 'em.

A large hand smacks my back, and I flash a scowl in the direction it came from. Torch meets my glower with a smirk. "You gonna fucking claim the bitch or just tease us?"

I blink, letting his word register through my lust-induced fog and peer around the room. Everyone's stopped what they're doing, nosily staring at Amelia and me. I was far too ensconced with my woman to notice a room bustling full of people. Clearly, she's not just another piece of ass to me; *she's my more.*

Blaze

With determination filling my irises, I declare loudly while staring Torch down. "Mine." I move my glare around the room, daring a motherfucker to say different. Would I kill to keep her or to make her mine? *I would.* She belongs to me, and I can't stand the notion of another trying to take her away, it makes me feel feral inside at the thought alone.

Reaching for her pants, I grab the material at the inside of her crotch and rip a giant hole there as well. I know Amelia would never be comfortable being on display for everyone, but I have to follow club rules to claim her. Nowhere does it say the brothers have to see her naked body, they just have to witness me fuck and claim her. It's club tradition, and I want her recognized as the real deal, to be respected as she deserves being my ol' lady.

Flicking the button on my jeans, Amelia's mouth pops open. She knows damn well that I'm serious, and I think she's in shock that I'm going to fuck her here and now. I move quickly, not wanting her to come to her senses and push me away. With my cock in my hand, I position myself at her entrance through the hole I ripped in her pants and thrust.

Her head flies back, a cry escaping her lips as I don't hold back. This is a claiming, not some sweet, soft fuck. We did that already this morning. This is so there's no doubt in anyone's mind who this pussy belongs to.

"Blaze!" she whimpers, and my hands move to her hips to hold her firm. The table scrapes loudly against the stained concrete floors with each thrust. I gaze at her, my stare full of ownership, yet submission. Not only does she belong to me, but I belong to her. She's the empress in my world, there's no doubt in my mind.

"*Mine*," I repeat, this time louder with a deadly threat lacing my tone. I stare intently into her eyes, making my intentions more than clear. Her legs wrap around my hips, her hands gripping around the sides of the square table to hold on. My gaze skirts around as sweat dots my brow, and I proclaim, "She's my motherfuckin' property. Anyone touches her, they'll lose their hand. Anyone fuc-cks with her, and I'll gut 'em." I growl, filled with intense pleasure as I thrust into my woman repeatedly.

She gasps, watching me wide-eyed. "Blaze?" she breathes.

I hear her unspoken question, and I nod.

Fire blazes in her irises as she sits up on my thrust. I had no idea she had upper body strength like that. Using my shoulders, she pulls herself onto me like a damn monkey. One of her dainty hands wraps around my throat. I don't know what in the hell to think, but I go with it. Using her thigh muscles, she squeezes me until I slow down. She peers into my eyes, completely serious, and declares, "*Mine!*" She squeezes my throat simultaneously, and I come so fucking hard.

Perfection.

My mouth dives in, taking hers as I pump her tight cunt full of my cum. Our tongues lash at each other. She fights me for control, but in the end, she submits and takes what I give her. Her pussy contracts around my length, and she cries out into my mouth as her orgasm rushes through her.

Going into this, I thought she was going to be an easy woman to break. I'd never imagined she'd come out of this ordeal as my ol' lady or that I'd be fucking gone for her. With that thought, I lean down to hold my jeans in one hand and move to carry her to my room. There's no way in hell I'm anywhere near finished with her.

The brothers hoot and cheer behind me. She's got a decent grip on me, so I use my other hand to throw up the bird on our way out.

Nosey fuckers.

"Your chariot awaits, Dr. Stone," Blaze whispers next to my ear as he comes up behind me. I'm outside for dismissal overseeing the students being picked up. It's been months since he took me initially, and every day like clockwork, he's here for me again.

His hand lands on my hip, and he squeezes. He knows I can't do PDA with students around, so he settles for that small way of showing the world that we're together. I know the thought of us together is crazy, but surprisingly, it works. Who am I kidding, it more than works. I'm head over heels for the brash man. I tried to fight it a little at first, but it didn't last. I couldn't when he'd show up at lunch every day and pin me over my desk to have his way. I didn't make it two days before giving in. I want to be with him, so why fight or ignore it?

"Is that so?" I tease, and he answers with a playful growl.

"I decided it's your turn to drive."

My mouth pops open, and I spin around, stunned. He's wearing a naughty grin. "Why do I think we're talking about different things?"

He shrugs and chuckles, "Guess you'll have to wait and see."

A smile breaks free. I couldn't hold it back if I tried.

His hand reaches out, and his finger gently brushes my jawline. "How was your day, babe?"

"It was okay; better now that you're here."

"And you get me for the entire weekend."

My eyes light up. "I do? I thought you had work."

He shrugs. "Plans change; besides, I have a surprise for you."

"Ohh, what is it?"

"We got the apartment you liked."

"What!" I exclaim, my heart thundering with excitement. We'd been apartment hunting, and I absolutely adored a place we saw on the outskirts of town. I had a small house before, but my lease was up, and Blaze was determined that we live together, so it seemed like the logical step to take together.

He nods, and I can't hold back from throwing my arms around his bulk. He squeezes me back, chuckling. "Turns out the manager could be persuaded to lower the rent too."

I pull back, my brows turning down. "Blaze, you didn't...hurt him, did you?"

He rolls his eyes, leaning in to press his forehead against mine. "Babe, I told you not to worry about shit."

"*Blaze...*"

He huffs. "Fine, once he realized I'm an Oath Keeper, he offered to let me stay free cause he knows the place will be safer."

"Oh, wow," I murmur, feeling guilty for imagining the worst.

He nods. "I told him no, that we'll pay, but no more than your last place. Turns out his son is a police officer, and he told him the Oath Keepers are an asset to have around."

I move to cup both of his cheeks; I meet his stare and smile. "Thank you, Blaze."

He presses a quick peck to my nose and mumbles, "Anything for you."

His reply makes my heart burst, and before I can overthink it, I proclaim for the first time, "I love you."

He grins, pulling my body into his embrace now that everyone's gone, and it's just us. "Babe..." He kisses my forehead. "I love you, too, beautiful. I have something for you."

"More?" I ask and walk wrapped in his arms to his bike. I've already locked up my office, and the janitor will finish securing the main doors when he's finished with his work.

"Yep." He reaches into his saddlebag, pulling out something that resembles the cut he's wearing. I've been learning the lingo of everything MC since we made it official. I don't want to ever embarrass him, and besides, I soak up whatever knowledge I can get.

"Is that...?" I trail off, and he nods, wearing his signature sexy grin I've come to love.

"Yep, it's your patch. P sewed it on herself."

"Wow." I've come to learn more than just the terminology, but also the meaning behind some of the things they do. "So, I guess there's no turning back now, huh?"

His head tilts, and he sends me that *are you kidding me* look he gets occasionally. "Babe, I thought you knew...there was no turning back from the very moment I laid eyes on ya. You'll always be mine."

"I love you," I repeat, this time much more confidently and put my arms through the holes of the leather vest.

He pulls it on me, snapping the button closed on the front. Once he's satisfied, he meets my stare. "I love you too, babe. Don't you ever forget it, either." And then he kisses me like I've never been kissed before. That's when I know *he means it.*

He's mine forever, and I'm his too.

The end.

I hope you loved reading about Blaze and his feisty principal. Thank you for taking a chance on another one of my alphas! I keep seeing so many people out there dogging on alpha men, and that's where Blaze's story was formed. I'm married to an alpha—I have been for fifteen years now—and I can tell you firsthand that people are painting them all wrong. They aren't bad men; they're strong-minded men who love and protect fiercely. A true alpha won't attempt to snuff out your light but hold you up when you need it. They're the type of man who will stand in front of you only to protect; otherwise, they stand BEHIND you to watch your back and help you succeed. I'm strong, independent, opinionated, outspoken, and hardheaded. It took a true alpha to tame me, but I tamed his ass too.

This book is for my husband—without him, I wouldn't be the same.

- Sapphire Knight

Website

www.authorsapphireknight.com

Facebook

www.facebook.com/AuthorSapphireKnight

BookBub

www.bookbub.com/profile/sapphire-knight

Made in the USA
Columbia, SC
18 February 2025

54013880R00143